A HOUSEBOAT

ON THE STYX

BEING SOME ACCOUNT
OF THE DIVERSE DOINGS
OF THE ASSOCIATED SHADES

Book I of The Associated Shades

John Kendrick Bangs
Illustrated by Peter Newell

A Houseboat on the Styx
Bangs, John Kendrick

Original publication, 1895
New edition, 2018

Published by The Writers of the Apocalypse
117 N Carbon Street, PMB 208
Marion, IL 62959
Find our books online at: http://woksprint.apocalypsewriters.com

Ebook ISBN:
ISBN Print: 978-1-944322-26-7
Digital: 978-1-944322-27-4

A HOUSEBOAT

ON THE STYX

CHAPTER I:

CHARON MAKES A DISCOVERY

CHARON, the ferryman of renown, was cruising slowly along the Styx one pleasant Friday morning not long ago, and as he paddled idly on he chuckled mildly to himself as he thought of the monopoly in ferriage which in the course of years he had managed to build up.

"It's a great thing," he said, with a smirk of satisfaction, "it's a great thing to be the go-between between two states of being; to have the exclusive franchise to export and import shades from one state to the other, and withal to have had as clean a record as mine has been. Valuable as is my franchise, I never corrupted a public official in my life, and—"

Here Charon stopped his soliloquy and his boat simultaneously. As he rounded one of the many turns in the river a singular object met his gaze, and one, too, that filled him with misgiving. It was another craft, and that was a thing not to be tolerated. Had he, Charon, owned the exclusive right of way on the Styx all these years to have it disputed here in the closing decade of the Nineteenth Century? Had not he dealt satisfactorily with all, whether it was in the line of ferriage or in the providing of boats for pleasure-trips up the river? Had he not received expressions of satisfaction, indeed, from the most exclusive families of Hades with the very select series of picnics he had given at Charon's Glen Island? No wonder, then, that the queer-looking boat that met his gaze, moored in a shady nook on the dark side of the river, filled him with dismay.

"Blow me for a landlubber if I like that!" he said, in a hardly audible whisper. "And shiver my timbers if I don't find out what she's there for. If anybody thinks he can run an opposition line to mine on this river he's mightily mistaken. If it comes to competition, I can carry shades for nothing and still quaff the B. & G. yellow-label benzine three times a day without experiencing a financial panic. I'll show 'em a thing or two if they attempt to rival me. And what a boat! It looks for all the world like a Florentine barn on a canal-boat."

Charon paddled up to the side of the craft, and, standing up in the middle of his boat, cried out, "Ship ahoy!"

There was no answer, and the Ferryman hailed her again. Receiving no response to his second call, he resolved to investigate for himself; so, fastening his own boat to the stern-post of the stranger, he clambered on board. If he was astonished as he sat in his ferry-boat, he was paralyzed when he cast his eye over the unwelcome vessel he had boarded. He stood for at least two minutes rooted to the spot. His eye swept over a long, broad deck, the polish of which resembled that of a ball-room floor. Amidships, running from three-quarters aft to three-quarters forward, stood a structure that in its lines resembled, as Charon had intimated, a barn, designed by an architect enamoured of Florentine simplicity; but in its construction the richest of woods had been used, and in its interior arrangement and adornment nothing more palatial could be conceived.

"What's the blooming thing for?" said Charon, more dismayed than ever. "If they start another line with a craft like this, I'm very much afraid I'm done for after all. I wouldn't take a boat like mine myself if there was a floating palace like this going the same way. I'll have to see the Commissioners about this, and find out what it all means. I suppose it'll cost me a pretty penny, too, confound them!"

A prey to these unhappy reflections, Charon investigated further, and the more he saw the less he liked it. He was about to encounter opposition, and an opposition which was apparently backed by persons of great wealth—perhaps the Commissioners themselves. It was a consoling thought that he had saved enough money in the course of his career to enable him to live in comfort all his days, but this was not really what Charon was after. He wished to acquire enough to retire and become one of the smart set. It had been done in that section of the universe which lay on the bright side of the Styx, why not, therefore, on the other, he asked.

"I'm pretty well connected even if I am a boatman," he had been known to say. "With Chaos for a grandfather, and Erebus and Nox for parents, I've just as good blood in my veins as anybody in Hades. The Noxes are a mighty fine family, not as bright as the Days, but older; and we're poor—that's it, poor—and it's money makes caste these days. If I had millions, and owned a railroad, they'd call me a yacht-owner. As I haven't, I'm only a boatman. Bah! Wait and see! I'll be giving swell functions myself some day, and these upstarts will be on their knees before me begging to be asked. Then I'll get up a little aristocracy of my own, and I won't let a soul into it whose name isn't mentioned in the Grecian mythologies. Mention in Burke's peerage and the Élite directories of America won't admit anybody to Commodore Charon's house unless there's some other mighty good reason for it."

Foreseeing an unhappy ending to all his hopes, the old man clambered sadly back into his ancient vessel and paddled off into the darkness. Some hours later, returning with a large company of new arrivals, while counting up the profits of the day Charon again caught sight of the new craft, and saw that it was brilliantly lighted and thronged with the most famous citizens of the Erebean country. Up in the bow was a spirit band discoursing music of the sweetest sort. Merry peals of laughter rang out over the dark waters of the Styx. The clink of glasses and the popping of corks punctuated the music with a frequency which would have delighted the soul of the most ardent lover of commas, all of which so overpowered the grand master boatman of the Stygian Ferry Company that he dropped three oboli and an American dime, which he carried as a pocket-piece, overboard. This, of course, added to his woe; but it was forgotten in an instant, for someone on the new boat had turned a search-light directly upon Charon himself, and simultaneously hailed the master of the ferry-boat.

"Charon!" cried the shade in charge of the light. "Charon, ahoy!"

"Ahoy yourself!" returned the old man, paddling his craft close up to the stranger. "What do you want?"

"You," said the shade. "The house committee want to see you right away."

"What for?" asked Charon, cautiously.

"I'm sure I don't know. I'm only a member of the club, and house committees never let mere members know anything about their plans. All I know is that you are wanted," said the other.

"Who are the house committee?" queried the Ferryman.

"Sir Walter Raleigh, Cassius, Demosthenes, Blackstone, Doctor Johnson, and Confucius," replied the shade.

"Tell 'em I'll be back in an hour," said Charon, pushing off. "I've got a cargo of shades on board consigned to various places up the river. I've promised to get 'em all through tonight, but I'll put on a couple of extra paddles—two of the new arrivals are working their passage this trip—and it won't take as long as usual. What boat is this, anyhow?"

"The *Nancy Nox*, of Erebus."

"Thunder!" cried Charon, as he pushed off and proceeded on his way up the river. "Named after my mother! Perhaps it'll come out all right yet."

More hopeful of mood, Charon, aided by the two dead-head passengers, soon got through with his evening's work, and in less than an hour was back seeking admittance, as requested, to the company of Sir Walter Raleigh and his fellow-members on the house committee. He was received by these worthies with considerable effusiveness, considering his position in society, and it warmed the cockles of his aged heart to note that Sir Walter, who had always been rather distant to him since he had carelessly upset that worthy and Queen Elizabeth in the middle of the Styx far back in the last century, permitted him to shake three fingers of his left hand when he entered the committee-room.

"How do you do, Charon?" said Sir Walter, affably. "We are very glad to see you."

"Thank you, kindly, Sir Walter," said the boatman. "I'm glad to hear those words, your honor, for I've been feeling very bad since I had the misfortune to drop your Excellency and her Majesty overboard. I never knew how it happened, sir, but happen it did, and but for her Majesty's kind assistance it might have been the worse for us. Eh, Sir Walter?"

The knight shook his head menacingly at Charon. Hitherto he had managed to keep it a secret that the Queen had rescued him from drowning upon that occasion by swimming ashore herself first and throwing Sir

Walter her ruff as soon as she landed, which he had used as a life-preserver.

"'Sh!" he said, *sotto voce*. "Don't say anything about that, my man."

"Very well, Sir Walter, I won't," said the boatman; but he made a mental note of the knight's agitation, and perceived a means by which that illustrious courtier could be made useful to him in his scheming for social advancement.

"I understood you had something to say to me," said Charon, after he had greeted the others.

"We have," said Sir Walter. "We want you to assume command of this boat."

The old fellow's eyes lighted up with pleasure.

"You want a captain, eh?" he said.

"No," said Confucius, tapping the table with a diamond-studded chop-stick. "No. We want a—er—what the deuce is it they call the functionary, Cassius?"

"Senator, I think," said Cassius.

Demosthenes gave a loud laugh.

"Your mind is still running on senatorships, my dear Cassius. That is quite evident," he said. "This is not one of them, however. The title we wish Charon to assume is neither captain nor senator; it is janitor."

"What's that?" asked Charon, a little disappointed. "What does a janitor have to do?"

"He has to look after things in the house," explained Sir Walter. "He's a sort of proprietor by proxy. We want you to take charge of the house, and see to it that the boat is kept shipshape."

"Where is the house?" queried the astonished boat-man.

"This is it," said Sir Walter. "This is the house, and the boat too. In fact, it is a houseboat."

"Then it isn't a new-fangled scheme to drive me out of business?" said Charon, warily.

"Not at all," returned Sir Walter. "It's a new-fangled scheme to set you up in business. We'll pay you a large salary, and there won't be much to do. You are the best man for the place, because, while you don't know much about houses, you do know a great deal about boats, and the boat part is the most important part of a houseboat. If the boat sinks, you can't save the house; but if the house burns, you may be able to save the boat. See?"

"I think I do, sir," said Charon.

"Another reason why we want to employ you for janitor," said Confucius, "is that our club wants to be in direct communication with both sides of the Styx; and we think you as janitor would be able to make better arrangements for transportation with yourself as boat-man, than some other man as janitor could make with you."

"Spoken like a sage," said Demosthenes.

"Furthermore," said Cassius, "occasionally we shall want to have this boat towed up or down the river, ac-cording to the house committee's pleasure, and we think it would be well to have a janitor who has some influ-ence with the towing company which you represent."

"Can't this boat be moved without towing?" asked Charon.

"No," said Cassius.

"And I'm the only man who can tow it, eh?"

"You are," said Blackstone. "Worse luck."

"And you want me to be janitor on a salary of what?"

"A hundred oboli a month," said Sir Walter, uneasily.

"Very well, gentlemen," said Charon. "I'll accept the office on a salary of two hundred oboli a month, with Saturdays off."

The committee went into executive session for five minutes, and on their return informed Charon that in behalf of the Associated Shades they accepted his offer.

"In behalf of what?" the old man asked.

"The Associated Shades," said Sir Walter. "The swellest organization in Hades, whose new houseboat you are now on board of. When shall you be ready to begin work?"

"Right away," said Charon, noting by the clock that it was the hour of midnight. "I'll start in right away, and as it is now Saturday morning, I'll begin by taking my day off."

Charon discovers a strange-looking craft

Charon is received by the House Committee

CHAPTER II:

A DISPUTED AUTHORSHIP

"HOW ARE YOU, Charon?" said Shakespeare, as the janitor assisted him on board. "Anyone here tonight?"

"Yes, sir," said Charon. "Lord Bacon is up in the library, and Doctor Johnson is down in the billiard-room, playing pool with Nero."

"Ha-ha!" laughed Shakespeare. "Pool, eh? Does Nero play pool?"

"Not as well as he does the fiddle, sir," said the janitor, with a twinkle in his eye.

Shakespeare entered the house and tossed up an obolus. "Heads—Bacon; tails—pool with Nero and Johnson," he said.

The coin came down with heads up, and Shakespeare went into the pool room, just to show the Fates that he didn't care a tuppence for their verdict as registered through the obolus. It was a peculiar custom of Shakespeare's to toss up a coin to decide questions of little consequence, and then do the thing the coin decided he should not do. It showed, in Shakespeare's estimation, his entire independence of those dull persons who supposed that in them was centered the destiny of all mankind. The Fates, however, only smiled at these little acts of rebellion, and it was common gossip in Erebus that one of the trio had told the Furies that they had observed Shakespeare's tendency to kick over the traces, and always acted accordingly. They never let the coin fall so as to decide a question the way they wanted it, so that unwittingly the great dramatist did their will after all. It was a part of their plan that upon this occasion Shakespeare should play pool with Doctor Johnson and the Emperor Nero, and hence it was that the coin bade him repair to the library and chat with Lord Bacon.

"Hullo, William," said the Doctor, pocketing three balls on the break. "How's our little Swanlet of Avon this afternoon?"

"Worn out," Shakespeare replied. "I've been hard at work on a play this morning, and I'm tired."

"All work and no play makes Jack a dull boy," said Nero, grinning broadly.

"You are a bright spirit," said Shakespeare, with a sigh. "I wish I had thought to work you up into a tragedy."

"I've often wondered why you didn't," said Doctor Johnson. "He'd have made a superb tragedy, Nero would. I don't believe there was any kind of a crime he left uncommitted. Was there, Emperor?"

"Yes. I never wrote an English dictionary," returned the Emperor, dryly. "I've murdered everything but English, though."

"I could have made a fine tragedy out of you," said Shakespeare. "Just think what a dreadful climax for a tragedy it would be, Johnson, to have Nero, as the curtain fell, playing a violin solo."

"Pretty good," returned the Doctor. "But what's the use of killing off your audience that way? It's better business to let 'em live, I say. Suppose Nero gave a London audience that little musicale he provided at Queen Elizabeth's Wednesday night. How many purely mortal beings, do you think, would have come out alive?"

"Not one," said Shakespeare. "I was mighty glad that night that we were an immortal band. If it had been possible to kill us we'd have died then and there."

"That's all right," said Nero, with a significant shake of his head. "As my friend Bacon makes Ingo say, 'Beware, my lord, of jealousy.' You never could play a garden hose, much less a fiddle."

"What do you mean my attributing those words to Bacon?" demanded Shakespeare, getting red in the face.

"Oh, come now, William," remonstrated Nero. "It's all right to pull the wool over the eyes of the mortals. That's what they're there for; but as for us—we're all in the secret here. What's the use of putting on nonsense with us?"

"We'll see in a minute what the use is," retorted the Avonian. "We'll have Bacon down here." Here he touched an electric button, and Charon came in answer.

"Charon, bring Doctor Johnson the usual glass of

ale. Get some ice for the Emperor, and ask Lord Bacon to step down here a minute."

"I don't want any ice," said Nero.

"Not now," retorted Shakespeare, "but you will in a few minutes. When we have finished with you, you'll want an iceberg. I'm getting tired of this idiotic talk about not having written my own works. There's one thing about Nero's music that I've never said, because I haven't wanted to hurt his feelings, but since he has chosen to cast aspersions upon my honesty I haven't any hesitation in saying it now. I believe it was one of his fiddlings that sent Nature into convulsions and caused the destruction of Pompeii—so there! Put that on your music rack and fiddle it, my little Emperor."

Nero's face grew purple with anger, and if Shakespeare had been anything but a shade he would have fared ill, for the enraged Roman, poising his cue on high as though it were a lance, hurled it at the impertinent dramatist with all his strength, and with such accuracy of aim withal that it pierced the spot beneath which in life the heart of Shakespeare used to beat.

"Good shot," said Doctor Johnson, nonchalantly. "If you had been a mortal, William, it would have been the end of you."

"You can't kill me," said Shakespeare, shrugging his shoulders. "I know seven dozen actors in the United States who are trying to do it, but they can't. I wish they'd try to kill a critic once in a while instead of me, though," he added. "I went over to Boston one night last week, and, unknown to anybody, I waylaid a fellow who was to play Hamlet that night. I drugged him, and went to the theatre and played the part myself. It was the coldest house you ever saw in your life. When the audience did applaud, it sounded like an ice-man chopping up ice with a small pick. Several times I looked up at the galleries to see if there were not icicles growing on them, it was so cold. Well, I did the best could with the part, and next morning watched curiously for the criticisms."

"Favorable?" asked the Doctor.

"They all dismissed me with a line," said the dramatist. "Said my conception of the part was not Shakespearian. And that's criticism!"

"No," said the shade of Emerson, which had strolled in while Shakespeare was talking, "that isn't criticism; that's Boston."

"Who discovered Boston, anyhow?" asked Doctor Johnson. "It wasn't Columbus, was it?"

"Oh no," said Emerson. "Old Governor Winthrop is to blame for that. When he settled at Charlestown he saw the old Indian town of Shawmut across the Charles."

"And Shawmut was the Boston microbe, was it?" asked Johnson.

"Yes," said Emerson.

"Spelt with a P, I suppose?" said Shakespeare. "P-S-H-A-W, Pshaw, M-U-T, mut, Pshawmut, so called because the inhabitants are always muttering pshaw. Eh?"

"Pretty good," said Johnson. "I wish I'd said that."

"Well, tell Boswell," said Shakespeare. "He'll make

you say it, and it'll be all the same in a hundred years."

Lord Bacon, accompanied by Charon and the ice for Nero and the ale for Doctor Johnson, appeared as Shakespeare spoke. The philosopher bowed stiffly at Doctor Johnson, as though he hardly approved of him, extended his left hand to Shakespeare, and stared coldly at Nero.

"Did you send for me, William?" he asked, languidly.

"I did," said Shakespeare. "I sent for you because this imperial violinist here says that you wrote *Othello*."

"What nonsense," said Bacon. "The only plays of yours I wrote were *Ham*—"

"Sh!" said Shakespeare, shaking his head madly. "Hush. Nobody's said anything about that. This is purely a discussion of *Othello*."

"The fiddling ex-Emperor Nero," said Bacon, loudly enough to be heard all about the room, "is mistaken when he attributes *Othello* to me."

"Aha, Master Nero!" cried Shakespeare triumphantly. "What did I tell you?"

"Then I erred, that is all," said Nero. "And I apologize. But really, my Lord," he added, addressing Bacon, "I fancied I detected your fine Italian hand in that."

"No. I had nothing to do with the *Othello*," said Bacon. "I never really knew who wrote it."

"Never mind about that," whispered Shakespeare. "You've said enough."

"That's good too," said Nero, with a chuckle. "Shakespeare here claims it as his own."

Bacon smiled and nodded approvingly at the blushing Avonian.

"Will always was having his little joke," he said. "Eh, Will? How we fooled 'em on *Hamlet*, eh, my boy? Ha-ha-ha! It was the greatest joke of the century."

"Well, the laugh is on you," said Doctor Johnson. "If you wrote *Hamlet* and didn't have the sense to acknowledge it, you present to my mind a closer resemblance to Simple Simon than to Socrates. For my part, I don't believe you did write it, and I do believe that Shakespeare did. I can tell that by the spelling in the original edition."

"Shakespeare was my stenographer, gentlemen," said Lord Bacon. "If you want to know the whole truth, he did write *Hamlet*, literally. But it was at my dictation."

"I deny it," said Shakespeare. "I admit you gave me a suggestion now and then so as to keep it dull and heavy in spots, so that it would seem more like a real tragedy than a comedy punctuated with deaths, but beyond that you had nothing to do with it."

"I side with Shakespeare," put in Emerson. "I've seen his autographs, and no sane person would employ a man who wrote such a villanously bad hand as an amanuensis. It's no use, Bacon, we know a thing or two. I'm a New-Englander, I am."

"Well," said Bacon, shrugging his shoulders as though the results of the controversy were immaterial to him, "have it so if you please. There isn't any money in Shakespeare these days, so what's the use of quarrelling? I wrote *Hamlet*, and Shakespeare knows it. Others know it. Ah, here comes Sir Walter Raleigh. We'll leave it to him. He was cognizant of the whole affair."

"I leave it to nobody," said Shakespeare, sulkily.

"What's the trouble?" asked Raleigh, sauntering up and taking a chair under the cue-rack. "Talking politics?"

"Not we," said Bacon. "It's the old question about the authorship of *Hamlet*. Will, as usual, claims it for himself. He'll be saying he wrote Genesis next."

"Well, what if he does?" laughed Raleigh. "We all know Will and his droll ways."

"No doubt," put in Nero. "But the question of *Hamlet* always excites him so that we'd like to have it settled once and for all as to who wrote it. Bacon says you know."

"I do," said Raleigh.

"Then settle it once and for all," said Bacon. "I'm rather tired of the discussion myself."

"Shall I tell 'em, Shakespeare?" asked Raleigh.

"It's immaterial to me," said Shakespeare, airily. "If you wish—only tell the truth."

"Very well," said Raleigh, lighting a cigar. "I'm not ashamed of it. I wrote the thing myself."

There was a roar of laughter which, when it subsided, found Shakespeare rapidly disappearing through the door, while all the others in the room ordered various beverages at the expense of Lord Bacon.

"Good shot," said Doctor Johnson, nonchalantly.

Lord Bacon, accompanied by Charon, appeared.

CHAPTER III:

WASHINGTON GIVES A DINNER

IT WAS Washington's Birthday, and the gentleman who had the pleasure of being Father of his Country decided to celebrate it at the Associated Shades' floating palace on the Styx, as the Elysium *Weekly Gossip*, "a Journal of Society," called it, by giving a dinner to a select number of friends. Among the invited guests were Baron Munchausen, Doctor Johnson, Confucius, Napoleon Bonaparte, Diogenes, and Ptolemy. Boswell was also present, but not as a guest. He had a table off to one side all to himself, and upon it there were no china plates, silver spoons, knives, forks, and dishes of fruit, but pads, pens, and ink in great quantity. It was evident that Boswell's reportorial duties did not end with his labors in the mundane sphere.

The dinner was set down to begin at seven o'clock, so that the guests, as was proper, sauntered slowly in between that hour and eight. The menu was particularly choice, the shades of countless canvas-back ducks, terrapin, and sheep having been called into requisition, and cooked by no less a person than Brillat-Savarin, in the hottest oven he could find in the famous cooking establishment superintended by the government. Washington was on hand early, sampling the olives and the celery and the wines, and giving to Charon final instructions as to the manner in which he wished things served.

The first guest to arrive was Confucius, and after him came Diogenes, the latter in great excitement over having discovered a comparatively honest man, whose name, however, he had not been able to ascertain, though he was under the impression that it was something like Burpin, or Turpin, he said.

At eight the brilliant company was arranged comfortably about the board. An orchestra of five, under the leadership of Mozart, discoursed sweet music behind a screen, and the feast of reason and flow of soul began.

"This is a great day," said Doctor Johnson, assisting himself copiously to the olives.

"Yes," said Columbus, who was also a guest—"yes, it is a great day, but it isn't a marker to a little day in October I wot of."

"Still sore on that point?" queried Confucius, trying the edge of his knife on the shade of a salted almond.

"Oh no," said Columbus, calmly. "I don't feel jealous of Washington. He is the Father of his Country and I am not. I only discovered the orphan. I knew the country before it had a father or a mother. There wasn't anybody who was willing to be even a sister to it when I knew it. But G. W. here took it in hand, groomed it down, spanked it when it needed it, and started it off on the career which has made it worthwhile for me to let my name be known in connection with it. Why should I be jealous of him?"

"I am sure I don't know why anybody anywhere should be jealous of anybody else anyhow," said Diogenes. "I never was and I never expect to be. Jealousy is a quality that is utterly foreign to the nature of an honest man. Take my own case, for instance. When I was what they call alive, how did I live?"

"I don't know," said Doctor Johnson, turning his head as he spoke so that Boswell could not fail to hear. "I wasn't there."

Boswell nodded approvingly, chuckled slightly, and put the Doctor's remark down for publication in *The Gossip*.

"You're doubtless right, there," retorted Diogenes. "What you don't know would fill a circulating library. Well—I lived in a tub. Now, if I believed in envy, I suppose you think I'd be envious of people who live in brownstone fronts with back yards and mortgages, eh?"

"I'd rather live under a mortgage than in a tub," said Bonaparte, contemptuously.

"I know you would," said Diogenes. "Mortgages never bothered you—but I wouldn't. In the first place, my tub was warm. I never saw a house with a brownstone front that was, except in summer, and then the owner cursed it because it was so. My tub had no plumbing in it to get out of order. It hadn't any flights of stairs in it that had to be climbed after dinner, or late at night when I came home from the club. It had no front door with a wandering key-hole calculated to elude the key ninety-nine times out of every hundred efforts to bring the two together and reconcile their differences, in order that their owner may get into his own house late at night. It wasn't chained down to any particular neighborhood, as are most brownstone fronts. If the neighborhood ran down, I could move my tub off into a better neighborhood, and it never lost value through the deterioration of its location. I never had to pay taxes on it, and no burglar was ever so hard up that he thought of breaking into my habitation to rob me. So why should I be jealous of the brownstone-house dwellers? I am a philosopher, gentlemen. I tell you, philosophy is the thief of jealousy, and I had the good-luck to find it out early in life."

"There is much in what you say," said Confucius. "But there's another side to the matter. If a man is an aristocrat by nature, as I was, his neighborhood never could run down. Wherever he lived would be the swell section, so that really your last argument isn't worth a stewed icicle."

"Stewed icicles are pretty good, though," said Baron Munchausen, with an ecstatic smack of his lips. "I've eaten them many a time in the polar regions."

"I have no doubt of it," put in Doctor Johnson. "You've eaten fried pyramids in Africa, too, haven't you?"

"Only once," said the Baron, calmly. "And I can't say I enjoyed them. They are rather heavy for the digestion."

"That's so," said Ptolemy. "I've had experience with pyramids myself."

"You never ate one, did you, Ptolemy?" queried Bonaparte.

"Not raw," said Ptolemy, with a chuckle. "Though I've been tempted many a time to call for a second joint of the Sphinx."

There was a laugh at this, in which all but Baron Munchausen joined.

"I think it is too bad," said the Baron, as the laughter subsided—"I think it is very much too bad that you shades have brought mundane prejudice with you into this sphere. Just because some people with finite minds profess to disbelieve my stories, you think it well to be skeptical yourselves. I don't care, however, whether you believe me or not. The fact remains that I have eaten one fried pyramid and countless stewed icicles, and the stewed icicles were finer than any diamond-back rat Confucius ever had served at a state banquet."

"Where's Shakespeare tonight?" asked Confucius, seeing that the Baron was beginning to lose his temper, and wishing to avoid trouble by changing the subject. "Wasn't he invited, General?"

"Yes," said Washington, "he was invited, but he couldn't come. He had to go over the river to consult with an autograph syndicate they've formed in New York. You know, his autographs sell for about one thousand dollars apiece, and they're trying to get up a scheme whereby he shall contribute an autograph a week to the syndicate, to be sold to the public. It seems like a rich scheme, but there's one thing in the way. Posthumous autographs haven't very much of a market, because the mortals can't be made to believe that they are genuine; but the syndicate has got a man at work trying to get over that. These Yankees are a mighty inventive lot, and they think perhaps the scheme can be worked. The Yankee *is* an inventive genius."

"It was a Yankee invented that tale about your not being able to prevaricate, wasn't it, George?" asked Diogenes.

Washington smiled acquiescence, and Doctor Johnson returned to Shakespeare.

"I'd rather have a morning-glory vine than one of Shakespeare's autographs," said he. "They are far prettier, and quite as legible."

"Mortals wouldn't," said Bonaparte.

"What fools they be!" chuckled Johnson.

At this point the canvas-back ducks were served, one whole shade of a bird for each guest.

"Fall to, gentlemen," said Washington, gazing hungrily at his bird. "When canvas-back ducks are on the table conversation is not required of any one."

"It is fortunate for us that we have so considerate a host," said Confucius, unfastening his robe and preparing to do justice to the fare set before him. "I have dined often, but never before with one who was willing to let me eat a bird like this in silence. Washington, here's to you. May your life be checkered with birthdays, and may ours be equally well supplied with feasts like this at your expense!"

The toast was drained, and the diners fell to as requested.

"They're great, aren't they?" whispered Bonaparte to Munchausen.

"Well, rather," returned the Baron. "I don't see why the mortals don't erect a statue to the canvas-back."

"Did anybody at this board ever have as much canvas-back duck as he could eat?" asked Doctor Johnson.

"Yes," said the Baron. "I did. Once."

"Oh, you!" sneered Ptolemy. "You've had everything."

"Except the mumps," retorted Munchausen. "But, honestly, I did once have as much canvas-back duck as I could eat."

"It must have cost you a million," said Bonaparte. "But even then they'd be cheap, especially to a man like yourself who could perform miracles. If I could have performed miracles with the ease which was so characteristic of all your efforts, I'd never have died at St. Helena."

"What's the odds where you died?" said Doctor Johnson. "If it hadn't been at St. Helena it would have been somewhere else, and you'd have found death as stuffy in one place as in another."

"Don't let's talk of death," said Washington. "I am sure the Baron's tale of how he came to have enough canvas-back is more diverting."

"I've no doubt it is more perverting," said Johnson.

"It happened this way," said Munchausen. "I was out for sport, and I got it. I was alone, my servant having fallen ill, which was unfortunate, since I had always left the filling of my cartridge-box to him, and underestimated its capacity. I started at six in the morning, and, not having hunted for several months, was not in very good form, so, no game appearing for a time, I took a few practice shots, trying to snip off the slender tops of the pine-trees that I encountered with my bullets, succeeding tolerably well for one who was a little rusty, bringing down ninety-nine out of the first one hundred and one, and missing the remaining two by such a close margin that they swayed to and fro as though fanned by a slight breeze. As I fired my one hundred and first shot what should I see before me but a flock of these delicate birds floating upon the placid waters of the bay!"

"Was this the Bay of Biscay, Baron?" queried Columbus, with a covert smile at Ptolemy.

"I counted them," said the Baron, ignoring the question, "and there were just sixty-eight. 'Here's a chance for the record, Baron,' said I to myself, and then I made ready to shoot them. Imagine my dismay, gentlemen, when I discovered that while I had plenty of powder left I had used up all my bullets. Now, as you may imagine, to a man with no bullets at hand, the sight of sixty-eight fat canvas-backs is hardly encouraging, but I was resolved to have every one of those birds; the question was, how shall I do it? I never can think on water, so I paddled quietly ashore and began to reflect. As I lay there deep in thought, I saw lying upon the beach before me a superb oyster, and as reflection makes me hungry I seized upon the bivalve and swallowed him. As he went down something stuck in my throat, and, extricating it, what should it prove to be but a pearl of surpassing beauty.

"My first thought was to be content with my day's find. A pearl worth thousands surely was enough to satisfy the most ardent lover of sport; but on looking up I saw those ducks still paddling contentedly about, and I could not bring myself to give them up. Suddenly the idea came, the pearl is as large as a bullet, and fully as round. Why not use it? Then, as thoughts come to me in shoals, I next reflected, 'Ah—but this is only one bullet as against sixty-eight birds:' immediately a third thought came, 'why not shoot them all with a single bullet? It is possible, though not probable.' I snatched out a pad of paper and a pencil, made a rapid calculation based on the doctrine of chances, and proved to my own satisfaction that at some time or another within the following two weeks those birds would doubtless be sitting in a straight line and paddling about, Indian file, for an instant.

"I resolved to await that instant. I loaded my gun with the pearl and a sufficient quantity of powder to send the charge through every one of the ducks if, perchance, the first duck were properly hit. To pass over wearisome details, let me say that it happened just as I expected. I had one week and six days to wait, but finally the critical moment came. It was at midnight, but fortunately the moon was at the full, and I could see as plainly as though it had been day. The moment the ducks were in line I aimed and fired. They every one squawked, turned over, and died. My pearl had pierced the whole sixty-eight."

Boswell blushed.

"Ahem!" said Doctor Johnson. "It was a pity to lose the pearl."

"That," said Munchausen, "was the most interesting part of the story. I had made a second calculation in order to save the pearl. I deduced the amount of powder necessary to send the gem through sixty-seven and a half birds, and my deduction was strictly accurate. It fulfilled its mission of death on sixty-seven and was found buried in the heart of the sixty-eighth, a trifle discolored, but still a pearl, and worth a king's ransom."

Napoleon gave a derisive laugh, and the other guests sat with incredulity depicted upon every line of their faces.

"Do you believe that story yourself, Baron?" asked Confucius.

"Why not?" asked the Baron. "Is there anything improbable in it? Why should you disbelieve it? Look at our friend Washington here. Is there any one here who knows more about truth than he does? He doesn't disbelieve it. He's the only man at this table who treats me like a man of honor."

"He's host and has to," said Johnson, shrugging his shoulders.

"Well, Washington, let me put the direct question to you," said the Baron. "Say you aren't host and are under no obligation to be courteous. Do you believe I haven't been telling the truth?"

"My dear Munchausen," said the General, "don't ask me. I'm not an authority. I can't tell a lie—not even when I hear one. If you say your story is true, I must believe it, of course; but—ah—really, if I were you, I wouldn't tell it again unless I could produce the pearl and the wish-bone of one of the ducks at least."

Whereupon, as the discussion was beginning to grow acrimonious, Washington hailed Charon, and, ordering a boat, invited his guests to accompany him over into the world of realities, where they passed the balance of the evening haunting a vaudeville performance at one of the London music-halls.

The brilliant company was arranged
about the board.

An orchestra of five,
under the leadership of Mozart,
discoursed sweet music.

CHAPTER IV:

HAMLET MAKES A SUGGESTION

IT WAS a beautiful night on the Styx, and the silvery surface of that picturesque stream was dotted with gondolas, canoes, and other craft to an extent that made Charon feel like a highly prosperous savings-bank. Within the houseboat were gathered a merry party, some of whom were on mere pleasure bent, others of whom had come to listen to a debate, for which the entertainment committee had provided, between the venerable patriarch Noah and the late eminent showman P. T. Barnum. The question to be debated was upon the resolution passed by the committee, that "The Animals of the Antediluvian Period were Far More Attractive for Show Purposes than those of Modern Make," and, singular to relate, the affirmative was placed in the hands of Mr. Barnum, while to Noah had fallen the task of upholding the virtues of the modern freak. It is with the party on mere pleasure bent that we have to do upon this occasion. The proceedings of the debating-party are as yet in the hands of the official stenographer, but will be made public as soon as they are ready.

The pleasure-seeking group were gathered in the smoking-room of the club, which was, indeed, a smoking-room of a novel sort, the invention of an unknown shade, who had sold all the rights to the club through a third party, anonymously, preferring, it seemed, to remain in the Elysian world, as he had been in the mundane sphere, a mute inglorious Edison. It was a simple enough scheme, and, for a wonder, no one in the world of substantialities has thought to take it up. The smoke was stored in reservoirs, just as if it were so much gas or water, and was supplied on the hot-air furnace principle from a huge furnace in the hold of the houseboat, into which tobacco was shoveled by the hired man of the club night and day. The smoke from the furnace, carried through flues to the smoking-room, was there received and stored in the reservoirs, with each of which was connected one dozen rubber tubes, having at their ends amber mouth-pieces. Upon each of these mouth-pieces was arranged a small meter registering the amount of smoke consumed through it, and for this the consumer paid so much a foot. The value of the plan was threefold. It did away entirely with ashes, it saved to the consumers the value of the unconsumed tobacco that is represented by the unsmoked cigar ends, and it averted the possibility of cigarettes.

Enjoying the benefits of this arrangement upon the evening in question were Shakespeare, Cicero, Henry VIII., Doctor Johnson, and others. Of course Boswell was present too, for a moment, with his notebook, and this fact evoked some criticism from several of the smokers.

"You ought to be upstairs in the lecture room, Boswell," said Shakespeare, as the great biographer took his seat behind his friend the Doctor. "Doesn't the *Gossip* want a report of the debate?"

"It does," said Boswell; "but the *Gossip* endeavors always to get the most interesting items of the day, and Doctor Johnson has informed me that he expects to be unusually witty this evening, so I have come here."

"Excuse me for saying it, Boswell," said the Doctor, getting red in the face over this unexpected confession, "but, really, you talk too much."

"That's good," said Cicero. "Stick that down, Boz, and print it. It's the best thing Johnson has said this week."

Boswell smiled weakly, and said: "But, Doctor, you did say that, you know. I can prove it, too, for you told me some of the things you were going to say. Don't you remember, you were going to lead Shakespeare up to making the remark that he thought the English language was the greatest language in creation, whereupon you were going to ask him why he didn't learn it?"

"Get out of here, you idiot!" roared the Doctor. "You're enough to give a man apoplexy."

"You're not going back on the ladder by which you have climbed, are you, Samuel?" queried Boswell, earnestly.

"The wha-a-t?" cried the Doctor, angrily. "The ladder—on which I climbed? You? Great heavens! That it should come to this! ...Leave the room—instantly! Ladder! By all that is beautiful—the ladder upon which I, Samuel Johnson, the tallest person in letters, have climbed! Go! Do you hear?"

Boswell rose meekly, and, with tears coursing down his cheeks, left the room.

"That's one on you, Doctor," said Cicero, wrapping his toga about him. "I think you ought to order up three baskets of champagne on that."

"I'll order up three baskets full of Boswell's remains if he ever dares speak like that again!" retorted the Doctor, shaking with anger. "He—my ladder—why, it's ridiculous."

"Yes," said Shakespeare, dryly. "That's why we laugh."

"You were a little hard on him, Doctor," said Henry VIII. "He was a valuable man to you. He had a great eye for your greatness."

"Yes. If there's any feature of Boswell that's greater than his nose and ears, it's his great I," said the Doctor.

"You'd rather have him change his I to a U, I presume," said Napoleon, quietly.

The Doctor waved his hand impatiently. "Let's drop him," he said. "Dropping one's biographer isn't without precedent. As soon as any man ever got to know Napoleon well enough to write him up he sent him to the front, where he could get a little lead in his system."

"I wish I had had a Boswell all the same," said Shakespeare. "Then the world would have known the truth about me."

"It wouldn't if he'd relied on your word for it," retorted the Doctor. "Hullo! here's Hamlet."

As the Doctor spoke, in very truth the melancholy Dane appeared in the doorway, more melancholy of aspect than ever.

"What's the matter with you?" asked Cicero, addressing the new-comer. "Haven't you got that poison out of your system yet?"

"Not entirely," said Hamlet, with a sigh; "but it isn't that that's bothering me. It's Fate."

"We'll get out an injunction against Fate if you like," said Blackstone. "Is it persecution, or have you deserved it?"

"I think it's persecution," said Hamlet. "I never wronged Fate in my life, and why she should pursue me like a demon through all eternity is a thing I can't understand."

"Maybe Ophelia is back of it," suggested Doctor Johnson. "These women have a great deal of sympathy for each other, and, candidly, I think you behaved pretty rudely to Ophelia. It's a poor way to show your love for a young woman, running a sword through her father every night for pay, and driving the girl to suicide with equal frequency, just to show theatre-goers what a smart little Dane you can be if you try."

"'Tisn't me does all that," returned Hamlet. "I only did it once, and even then it wasn't as bad as Shakespeare made it out to be."

"I put it down just as it was," said Shakespeare, hotly, "and you can't dispute it."

"Yes, he can," said Yorick. "You made him tell Horatio he knew me well, and he never met me in his life."

"I never told Horatio anything of the sort," said Hamlet. "I never entered the graveyard even, and I can prove an alibi."

"And, what's more, he couldn't have made the remark the way Shakespeare has it, anyhow," said Yorick, "and for a very good reason. I wasn't buried in that graveyard, and Hamlet and I can prove an alibi for the skull, too."

"It was a good play, just the same," said Cicero.

"Very," put in Doctor Johnson. "It cured me of insomnia."

"Well, if you don't talk in your sleep, the play did a Christian service to the world," retorted Shakespeare. "But, really, Hamlet, I thought I did the square thing by you in that play. I meant to, anyhow; and if it has made you unhappy, I'm honestly sorry."

"Spoken like a man," said Yorick.

"I don't mind the play so much," said Hamlet, "but the way I'm represented by these fellows who play it is the thing that rubs me the wrong way. Why, I even hear that there's a troupe out in the western part of the United States that puts the thing on with three Hamlets, two ghosts, and a pair of blood-hounds. It's called the Uncle-Tom-Hamlet Combination, and instead of my falling in love with one crazy Ophelia, I am made to woo three dusky maniacs named Topsy on a canvas ice-floe, while the blood-hounds bark behind the scenes. What sort of treatment is that for a man of royal lineage?"

"It's pretty rough," said Napoleon. "As the poet ought to have said, 'Oh, Hamlet, Hamlet, what crimes are committed in thy name!'"

"I feel as badly about the play as Hamlet does," said Shakespeare, after a moment of silent thought. "I don't bother much about this wild Western business, though, because I think the introduction of the bloodhounds and the Topsies makes us both more popular in that region than we should be otherwise. What I object to is the way we are treated by these so-called first-class intellectual actors in London and other great cities. I've seen Hamlet done before a highly cultivated audience, and, by Jove, it made me blush."

"Me too," sighed Hamlet. "I have seen a man who had a walk on him that suggested spring-halt and locomotor ataxia combined impersonating my graceful self in a manner that drove me almost crazy. I've heard my 'To be or not to be' soliloquy uttered by a famous tragedian in tones that would make a graveyard yawn at mid-day, and if there was any way in which I could get even with that man I'd do it."

"It seems to me," said Blackstone, assuming for the moment a highly judicial manner—"it seems to me that Shakespeare, having got you into this trouble, ought to get you out of it."

"But how?" said Shakespeare, earnestly. "That's the point. Heaven knows I'm willing enough."

Hamlet's face suddenly brightened as though illuminated with an idea. Then he began to dance about the room with an expression of glee that annoyed Doctor

Johnson exceedingly.

"I wish Darwin could see you now," the Doctor growled. "A Kodak picture of you would prove his arguments conclusively."

"Rail on, O philosopher!" retorted Hamlet. "Rail on! I mind your railings not, for I the germ of an idea have got."

"Well, go quarantine yourself," said the Doctor. "I'd hate to have one of your idea microbes get hold of me."

"What's the scheme?" asked Shakespeare.

"You can write a play for *me*!" cried Hamlet. "Make it a farce-tragedy. Take the modern player for your hero, and let *me* play *him*. I'll bait him through four acts. I'll imitate his walk. I'll cultivate his voice. We'll have the first act a tank act, and drop the hero into the tank. The second act can be in a saw-mill, and we can cut his hair off on a buzz-saw. The third act can introduce a spile-driver with which to drive his hat over his eyes and knock his brains down into his lungs. The fourth act can be at Niagara Falls, and we'll send him over the falls; and for a grand climax we can have him guillotined just after he has swallowed a quart of prussic acid and a spoonful of powdered glass. Do that for me, William, and you are forgiven. I'll play it for six hundred nights in London, for two years in New York, and round up with a one-night stand in Boston."

"It sounds like a good scheme," said Shakespeare, meditatively. "What shall we call it?"

"Call it *Irving*," said Eugene Aram, who had entered. "I too have suffered."

"And let me be Hamlet's understudy," said Charles the First, earnestly.

"Done!" said Shakespeare, calling for a pad and pencil.

And as the sun rose upon the Styx the next morning the Bard of Avon was to be seen writing a comic chorus to be sung over the moribund tragedian by the shades of Charles, Aram, and other eminent deceased heroes of the stage, with which his new play of *Irving* was to be brought to an appropriate close.

This play has not as yet found its way upon the boards, but any enterprising manager who desires to consider it may address

> *Hamlet,*
> *The Houseboat,*
> *Hades-on-the-Styx.*

He is sure to get a reply by return mail, unless Mephistopheles interferes, which is not unlikely, since Mephistopheles is said to have been much pleased with the manner in which the eminent tragedian has put him before the British and American public.

Doctor Johnson in a rage

The melancholy Dane appeared.

CHAPTER V:

THE HOUSE COMMITTEE DISCUSS THE POETS

"THERE'S ONE thing this houseboat needs," wrote Homer in the complaint-book that adorned the centre-table in the reading-room, "and that is a Poets' Corner. There are smoking-rooms for those who smoke, billiard-rooms for those who play billiards, and a card-room for those who play cards. I do not smoke, I can't play billiards, and I do not know a trey of diamonds from a silver salver. All I can do is write po-etry. Why discriminate against me? By all means let us have a Poets' Corner, where a man can be inspired in peace."

For four days this entry lay in the book apparently unnoticed. On the fifth day the following lines, signed by Samson, appeared:

"I approve of Homer's suggestion. There should be a Poets' Corner here. Then the rest of us could have some comfort. While playing *vingt-et-un* with Diogenes in the card-room on Friday evening a poetic member of this club was taken with a most violent fancy, and it required the combined efforts of Diogenes and myself, assisted by the janitor, to remove the frenzied and objectionable member from the room. The habit some of our poets have acquired of giving way to their inspirations all over the clubhouse should be stopped, and I know of no better way to accomplish this desirable end than by the adoption of Homer's suggestion. Therefore I second the motion."

Of course the suggestion of two members so prominent as Homer and Samson could not well he ignored by the house committee, and it reluctantly took the subject in hand at an early meeting.

"I find here," said Demosthenes to the chairman, as the committee gathered, "a suggestion from Homer and Samson that this houseboat be provided with a Poets' Corner. I do not know that I approve of the suggestion myself, but in order to bring it before the committee for debate I am willing to make a motion that the request be granted."

"Excuse me," put in Doctor Johnson, "but where do you find that suggestion? 'Here' is not very definite. Where *is* 'here'?"

"In the complaint-book, which I hold in my hand," returned Demosthenes, putting a pebble in his mouth so that he might enunciate more clearly.

A frown ruffled the serenity of Doctor Johnson's brow.

"In the complaint-book, eh?" he said, slowly. "I

thought house committees were not expected to pay any attention to complaints in complaint-books. I never heard of its being done before."

"Well, I can't say that I have either," replied Demosthenes, chewing thoughtfully on the pebble, "but I suppose complaint-books are the places for complaints. You don't expect people to write serial stories or dialect poems in them, do you?"

"That isn't the point, as the man said to the assassin who tried to stab him with the hilt of his dagger," retorted Doctor Johnson, with some asperity. "Of course, complaint-books are for the reception of complaints— nobody disputes that. What I want to have determined is whether it is necessary or proper for the complaints to go further."

"I fancy we have a legal right to take the matter up," said Blackstone, wearily; "though I don't know of any precedent for such action. In all the clubs I have known the house committees have invariably taken the ground that the complaint-book was established to guard them against the annoyance of hearing complaints. This one, however, has been forced upon us by our secretary, and in view of the age of the complainants I think we cannot well decline to give them a specific answer. Respect for age is *de rigueur* at all times, like clean hands. I'll second the motion."

"I think the Poets' Corner entirely unnecessary," said Confucius. "This isn't a class organization, and we should resist any effort to make it or any portion of it so. In fact, I will go further and state that it is my opinion that if we do any legislating in the matter at all, we ought to discourage rather than encourage these poets. They are always littering the club up with themselves. Only last Wednesday I came here with a guest—no less a person than a recently deceased Emperor of China—and what was the first sight that greeted our eyes?"

"I give it up," said Doctor Johnson. "It must have been a catacornered sight, whatever it was, if the Emperor's eyes slanted like yours."

"No personalities, please, Doctor," said Sir Walter Raleigh, the chairman, rapping the table vigorously with the shade of a handsome gavel that had once adorned the Roman Senate-chamber.

"He's only a Chinaman!" muttered Johnson.

"What was the sight that greeted your eyes, Confucius?" asked Cassius.

"Omar Khayyam stretched over five of the most comfortable chairs in the library," returned Confucius; "and when I ventured to remonstrate with him he lost his temper, and said I'd spoiled the whole second volume of the Rubáiyát. I told him he ought to do his rubáiyátting at home, and he made a scene, to avoid which I hastened with my guest over to the billiard-room; and there, stretched at full length on the pool-table, was Robert Burns trying to write a sonnet on the cloth with chalk in less time than Villon could turn out another, with two lines start, on the billiard-table with the same writing materials. Now I ask you, gentlemen, if these things are to be tolerated? Are they not rather to be reprehended, whether I am a Chinaman or not?"

"What would you have us do, then?" asked Sir Walter Raleigh, a little nettled. "Exclude poets altogether? I was one, remember."

"Oh, but not much of one, Sir Walter," put in Doctor Johnson, deprecatingly.

"No," said Confucius. "I don't want them excluded, but they should be controlled. You don't let a shoemaker who has become a member of this club turn the library sofas into benches and go pegging away at bootmaking, so why should you let the poets turn the place into a verse factory? That's what I'd like to know."

"I don't know but what your point is well taken," said Blackstone, "though I can't say I think your parallels are very parallel. A shoemaker, my dear Confucius, is somewhat different from a poet."

"Certainly," said Doctor Johnson. "Very different— in fact, different enough to make a conundrum of the question—what is the difference between a shoemaker and a poet? One makes the shoes and the other shakes the muse—all the difference in the world. Still, I don't see how we can exclude the poets. It is the very democracy of this club that gives it life. We take in everybody—peer, poet, or what not. To say that this man shall not enter because he is this or that or the other thing would result in our ultimately becoming a class organization, which, as Confucius himself says, we are not and must not be. If we put out the poet to please the sage, we'll soon have to put out the sage to please the fool, and so on. We'll keep it up, once the precedent is established, until finally it will become a class club en-

tirely—a Plumbers' Club, for instance—and how absurd that would be in Hades! No, gentlemen, it can't be
done. The poets must and shall be preserved."

"What's the objection to class clubs, anyhow?"
asked Cassius. "I don't object to them. If we could have
had political organizations in my day I might not have
had to fall on my sword to get out of keeping an en-
gagement I had no fancy for. Class clubs have their uses."

"No doubt," said Demosthenes. "Have all the class
clubs you want, but do not make one of this. An Authors' Club, where none but authors are admitted, is a
good thing. The members learn there that there are other
authors than themselves. Poets' Clubs are a good thing;
they bring poets into contact with each other, and they
learn what a bore it is to have to listen to a poet reading
his own poem. Pugilists' Clubs are good; so are all other class clubs; but so also are clubs like our own, which
takes in all who are worthy. Here a poet can talk poetry
as much as he wants, but at the same time he hears
something besides poetry. We must stick to our original
idea."

"Then let us do something to abate the nuisance of
which I complain," said Confucius. "Can't we adopt a
house rule that poets must not be inspired between the
hours of 11 A.M. and 5 P.M., or in the evening after
eight; that any poet discovered using more than five
arm-chairs in the composition of a quatrain will be
charged two oboli an hour for each chair in excess of
that number; and that the billiard-marker shall be re-

quired to charge a premium of three times the ordinary fee for tables used by versifiers in lieu of writing-pads?"

"That wouldn't be a bad idea," said Sir Walter Raleigh. "I, as a poet would not object to that. I do all my work at home, anyhow."

"There's another phase of this business that we haven't considered yet, and it's rather important," said Demosthenes, taking a fresh pebble out of his bonbonnière. "That's in the matter of stationery. This club, like all other well-regulated clubs, provides its members with a suitable supply of writing materials. Charon informs me that the waste-baskets last week turned out forty-two reams of our best correspondence paper on which these poets had scribbled the first draft of their verses. Now I don't think the club should furnish the poets with the raw material for their poems any more than, to go back to Confucius's shoemaker, it should supply leather for our cobblers."

"What do you mean by raw material for poems?" asked Sir Walter, with a frown.

"Pen, ink, and paper. What else?" said Demosthenes.

"Doesn't it take brains to write a poem?" said Raleigh.

"Doesn't it take brains to make a pair of shoes?" retorted Demosthenes, swallowing a pebble in his haste.

"They've got a right to the stationery, though," put in Blackstone. "A clear legal right to it. If they choose to write poems on the paper instead of boring people to death with letters, as most of us do, that's their own affair."

"Well, they're very wasteful," said Demosthenes.

"We can meet that easily enough," observed Cassius. "Furnish each writing-table with a slate. I should think they'd be pleased with that. It's so much easier to rub out the wrong word."

"Most poets prefer to rub out the right word," growled Confucius. "Besides, I shall never consent to slates in this houseboat. The squeaking of the pencils would be worse than the poems themselves."

"That's true," said Cassius. "I never thought of that. If a dozen poets got to work on those slates at once, a fife corps wouldn't be a circumstance to them."

"Well, it all goes to prove what I have thought all along," said Doctor Johnson. "Homer's idea is a good one, and Samson was wise in backing it up. The poets need to be concentrated somewhere where they will not be a nuisance to other people, and where other people will not be a nuisance to them. Homer ought to have a place to compose in where the *vingt-et-un* players will not interrupt his frenzies, and, on the other hand, the *vingt-et-un* and other players should be protected from the wooers of the muse. I'll vote to have the Poets' Corner, and in it I move that Cassius's slate idea be carried out. It will be a great saving, and if the corner we select be far enough away from the other corners of the club, the squeaking of the slate-pencils need bother no one."

"I agree to that," said Blackstone. "Only I think it should be understood that, in granting the petition of the poets, we do not bind ourselves to yield to doctors and lawyers and shoemakers and plumbers in case they should each want a corner to themselves."

"A very wise idea," said Sir Walter. Whereupon the resolution was suitably worded, and passed unanimously.

Just where the Poets' Corner is to be located the members of the committee have not as yet decided, although Confucius is strongly in favor of having it placed in a dingy situated a quarter of a mile astern of the houseboat, and connected therewith by a slight cord, which can be easily cut in case the squeaking of the poets' slate-pencils becomes too much for the nervous system of the members who have no corner of their own.

Ejecting a frenzied poet from the card room.

The House Committee discuss the poets.

"And I, too," put in Baron Munchausen, "have frequently conversed with monkeys."

CHAPTER VI:

SOME THEORIES, DARWINIAN AND OTHERWISE

"I OBSERVE," said Doctor Darwin, looking up from a perusal of an asbestos copy of the *London Times*—"I observe that an American professor has discovered that monkeys talk. I consider that a very interesting fact."

"It undoubtedly is," observed Doctor Livingstone, "though hardly new. I never said anything about it over in the other world, but I discovered years ago in Africa that monkeys were quite as well able to hold a sustained conversation with each other as most men are."

"And I, too," put in Baron Munchausen, "have frequently conversed with monkeys. I made myself a master of their idioms during my brief sojourn in—ah—in—well, never mind where. I never could remember the names of places. The interesting point is that at one period of my life I was a master of the monkey language. I have even gone so far as to write a sonnet in

Simian, which was quite as intelligible to the uneducated as nine-tenths of the sonnets written in English or American."

"Do you mean to say that you could acquire the monkey accent?" asked Doctor Darwin, immediately interested.

"In most instances," returned the Baron, suavely, "though of course not in all. I found the same difficulty in some cases that the German or the Chinaman finds when he tries to speak French. A Chinaman can no more say Trocadéro, for instance, as the Frenchman says it, than he can fly. That peculiar throaty aspirate the Frenchman gives to the first syllable, as though it were spelled trhoque, is utterly beyond the Chinese—and beyond the American, too, whose idea of the tonsillar aspirate leads him to speak of the trochedeero, naturally falling back upon troches to help him out of his laryngeal difficulties."

"You ought to have been on the staff of *Punch*, Baron," said Thackeray, quietly. "That joke would have made you immortal."

"I *am* immortal," said the Baron. "But to return to our discussion of the Simian tongue: as I was saying, there were some little points about the accent that I could never get, and, as in the case of the German and Chinaman with the French language, the trouble was purely physical. When you consider that in polite Simian society most of the talkers converse while swinging by their tails from the limb of a tree, with a sort of droning accent, which results from their swaying to and fro, you will see at once why it was that I, deprived by nature of the necessary apparatus with which to suspend myself in mid-air, was unable to quite catch the quality which gives its chief charm to monkey-talk."

"I should hardly think that a man of your fertile resources would have let so small a thing as that stand in his way," said Doctor Livingstone. "When a man is able to make a reputation for himself like yours, in which material facts are never allowed to interfere with his doing what he sets out to do, he ought not to be daunted by the need of a tail. If you could make a cherry-tree grow out of a deer's head, I fail to see why you could not personally grow a tail, or anything else you might happen to need for the attainment of your ends."

"I was not so anxious to get the accent as all that," returned the Baron. "I don't think it is necessary for a man to make a monkey of himself just for the pleasure of mastering a language. Reasoning similarly, a man to master the art of braying in a fashion comprehensible to the jackass of average intellect should make a jackass of himself, cultivate his ears, and learn to kick, so as properly to punctuate his sentences after the manner of most conversational beasts of that kind."

"Then you believe that jackasses talk, too, do you?" asked Doctor Darwin.

"Why not?" said the Baron. "If monkeys, why not donkeys? Certainly they do. All creatures have some means of communicating their thoughts to each other. Why man in his conceit should think otherwise I don't know, unless it be that the birds and beasts in their conceit probably think that they alone of all the creatures in the world can talk."

"I haven't a doubt," said Doctor Livingstone, "that monkeys listening to men and women talking think they are only jabbering."

"They're not far from wrong in most cases if they do," said Doctor Johnson, who up to this time had been merely an interested listener. "I've thought that many a time myself."

"Which is perhaps, in a slight degree, a confirmation of my theory," put in Darwin. "If Doctor Johnson's mind runs in the same channels that the monkey's mind runs in, why may we not say that Doctor Johnson, being a man, has certain qualities of the monkey, and is therefore, in a sense, of the same strain?"

"You may say what you please," retorted Johnson, wrathfully, "but I'll make you prove what you say about me."

"I wouldn't if I were you," said Doctor Livingstone, in a peace-making spirit. "It would not be a pleasant task for you, compelling our friend to prove you descended from the ape. I should think you'd prefer to make him leave it unproved."

"Have monkeys Boswells?" queried Thackeray.

"I don't know anything about 'em," said Johnson, petulantly.

"No more do I," said Darwin, "and I didn't mean to be offensive, my dear Johnson. If I claim Simian ancestry for you, I claim it equally for myself."

"Well, I'm no snob," said Johnson, unmollified. "If

you want to brag about your ancestors, do it. Leave mine alone. Stick to your own genealogical orchard."

"Well, I believe fully that we are all descended from the ape," said Munchausen. "There isn't any doubt in my mind that before the flood all men had tails. Noah had a tail. Shem, Ham, and Japheth had tails. It's perfectly reasonable to believe it. The Ark in a sense proved it. It would have been almost impossible for Noah and his sons to construct the Ark in the time they did with the assistance of only two hands apiece. Think, however, of how fast they could work with the assistance of that third arm. Noah could hammer a clapboard on to the Ark with two hands while grasping a saw and cutting a new board or planing it off with his tail. So with the others. We all know how much a third hand would help us at times."

"But how do you account for its disappearance?" put in Doctor Livingstone. "Is it likely they would dispense with such a useful adjunct?"

"No, it isn't; but there are various ways of accounting for its loss," said Munchausen. "They may have overworked it building the Ark; Shem, Ham, or Japheth may have had his caught in the door of the Ark and cut off in the hurry of the departure; plenty of things may have happened to eliminate it. Men lose their hair and their teeth; why might not a man lose a tail? Scientists say that coming generations far in the future will be toothless and bald. Why may it not be that through causes unknown to us we are similarly deprived of something our forefathers had?"

"The only reason for man's losing his hair is that he wears a hat all the time," said Livingstone. "The Derby hat is the enemy of hair. It is hot, and dries up the scalp. You might as well try to raise watermelons in the Desert of Sahara as to try to raise hair under the modern hat. In fact, the modern hat is a furnace."

"Well, it's a mighty good furnace," observed Munchausen. "You don't have to put coal on the modern hat."

"Perhaps," interposed Thackeray, "the ancients wore their hats on their tails."

"Well, I have a totally different theory," said Johnson.

"You always did have," observed Munchausen.

"Very likely," said Johnson. "To be commonplace never was my ambition."

"What is your theory?" queried Livingstone.

"Well—I don't know," said Johnson, "if it be worth expressing."

"It may be worth sending by freight," interrupted Thackeray. "Let us have it."

"Well, I believe," said Johnson, "I believe that Adam was a monkey."

"He behaved like one," ejaculated Thackeray.

"I believe that the forbidden tree was a tender one, and therefore the only one upon which Adam was forbidden to swing by his tail," said Johnson.

"Clear enough—so far," said Munchausen.

"But that the possession of tails by Adam and Eve entailed a love of swinging thereby, and that they could not resist the temptation to swing from every limb in Eden, and that therefore, while Adam was off swinging on other trees, Eve took a swing on the forbidden tree; that Adam, returning, caught her in the act, and immediately gave way himself and swung," said Johnson.

"Then you eliminate the serpent?" queried Darwin.

"Not a bit of it," Johnson answered. "The serpent was the tail. Look at most snakes today. What are they but unattached tails?"

"They do look it," said Darwin, thoughtfully.

"Why, it's clear as day," said Johnson. "As punishment Adam and Eve lost their tails, and the tail itself was compelled to work for a living and do its own walking."

"I never thought of that," said Darwin. "It seems reasonable."

"It is reasonable," said Johnson.

"And the snakes of the present day?" queried Thackeray.

"I believe to be the missing tails of men," said Johnson. "Somewhere in the world is a tail for every man and woman and child. Where one's tail is no one can ever say, but that it exists simultaneously with its owner I believe. The abhorrence man has for snakes is directly attributable to his abhorrence for all things which have deprived him of something that is good. If Adam's tail had not tempted him to swing on the forbidden tree, we should all of us have been able through life to relax from business cares after the manner of the monkey, who is happy from morning until night."

"Well, I can't see that it does us any good to sit here and discuss this matter," said Doctor Livingstone. "We can't reach any conclusion. The only way to settle the matter, it seems to me, is to go directly to Adam, who is a member of this club, and ask him how it was."

"That's a great idea," said Thackeray, scornfully. "You'd look well going up to a man and saying, 'Excuse me, sir, but—ah—were you ever a monkey?'"

"To say nothing of catechizing a man on the subject of an old and dreadful scandal," put in Munchausen. "I'm surprised at you, Livingstone. African etiquette seems to have ruined your sense of propriety."

"I'd just as lief ask him," said Doctor Johnson. "Etiquette? Bah! What business has etiquette to stand in the way of human knowledge? Conventionality is the last thing men of brains should strive after, and I, for one, am not going to be bound by it."

Here, Doctor Johnson touched the electric bell and in an instant the shade of a buttons appeared.

"Boy, is Adam in the clubhouse today?" asked the sage.

"I'll go and see, sir," said the boy, and he immediately departed.

"Good boy that," said Thackeray.

"Yes; but the service in this club is dreadful, considering what we might have," said Darwin. "With Aladdin a member of this club, I don't see why we can't have his lamp with genii galore to respond. It certainly would be more economical."

"Boy, is Adam in the clubhouse today?"

"True; but I, for one, don't care to fool with genii," said Munchausen. "When one member can summon a servant who is strong enough to take another member and do him up in a bottle and cast him into the sea, I have no use for the system. Plain ordinary mortal shades are good enough for me."

As Munchausen spoke, the boy returned.

"Mr. Adam isn't here today, sir," he said, addressing Doctor Johnson. "And Charon says he's not likely to be here, sir, seeing as how his account is closed, not having been settled for three months."

"Good," said Thackeray. "I was afraid he was here. I don't want to have him asked about his Eden experiences in my behalf. That's personality."

"Well, then, there's only one other thing to do," said Darwin. "Munchausen claims to be able to speak Simian. He might seek out some of the prehistoric monkeys and put the question to them."

"No, thank you," said Munchausen. "I'm a little rusty in the language, and, besides, you talk like an idiot. You might as well speak of the human language as the Simian language. There are French monkeys who speak monkey French, African monkeys who talk the most barbarous kind of Zulu monkey patois, and Congo monkey slang, and so on. Let Johnson send his little Boswell out to drum up information. If there is anything to be found out he'll get it, and then he can tell it to us. Of course he may get it all wrong, but it will be entertaining, and we'll never know any difference."

Which seemed to the others a good idea, but whatever came of it I have not been informed.

Sir Walter Raleigh meeting Queen Elizabeth

CHAPTER VII:

A DISCUSSION AS TO LADIES' DAY

"**I MET** Queen Elizabeth just now on the Row," said Raleigh, as he entered the houseboat and checked his cloak.

"Indeed?" said Confucius. "What if you did? Other people have met Queen Elizabeth. There's nothing original about that."

"True; but she made a suggestion to me about this houseboat which I think is a good one. She says the women are all crazy to see the inside of it," said Raleigh.

"Thus proving that immortal woman is no different from mortal woman," retorted Confucius. "They want to see the inside of everything. Curiosity, thy name is woman."

"Well, I am sure I don't see why men should arrogate to themselves the sole right to an investigating turn of mind," said Raleigh, impatiently. "Why shouldn't the ladies want to see the inside of this clubhouse? It is a compliment to us that they should, and I for one am in favor of letting them, and I am going to propose that in the Ides of March we give a ladies' day here."

"Then I shall go South for my health in the Ides of March," said Confucius, angrily. "What on earth is a club for if it isn't to enable men to get away from their wives once in a while? When do people go to clubs? When they are on their way home—that's when; and the more a man's at home in his club, the less he's at home when he's at home. I suppose you'll be suggesting a children's day next, and after that a parrot's or a canary-bird's day."

"I had no idea you were such a woman-hater," said Raleigh, in astonishment. "What's the matter? Were you ever disappointed in love?"

"I? How absurd!" retorted Confucius, reddening. "The idea of *my* ever being disappointed in love! I never met the woman who could bring me to my knees, although I was married in the other world. What became of Mrs. C. I never inquired. She may be in China yet, for aught I know. I regard death as a divorce."

"Your wife must be glad of it," said Raleigh, somewhat ungallantly; for, to tell the truth, he was nettled by Confucius's demeanor. "I didn't know, however, but that since you escaped from China and came here to Hades you might have fallen in love with some spirit of an age subsequent to your own—Mary Queen of Scots, or Joan of Arc, or some other spook—who rejected you. I can't account for your dislike of women otherwise."

"Not I," said Confucius. "Hades would have a less classic name than it has for me if I were hampered with a family. But go along and have your ladies' day here, and never mind my reasons for preferring my own society to that of the fair sex. I can at least stay at home that day. What do you propose to do—throw open the house to the wives of members, or to all ladies, irrespective of their husbands' membership here?"

"I think the latter plan would be the better," said Raleigh. "Otherwise Queen Elizabeth, to whom I am indebted for the suggestion, would be excluded. She never married, you know."

"Didn't she?" said Confucius. "No, I didn't know it; but that doesn't prove anything. When I went to school we didn't study the history of the Elizabethan period. She didn't have absolute sway over England, then?"

"She had; but what of that?" queried Raleigh.

"Do you mean to say that she lived and died an old maid from choice?" demanded Confucius.

"Certainly I do," said Raleigh. "And why should I not tell you that?"

"For a very good and sufficient reason," retorted Confucius, "which is, in brief, that I am not a marine. I may dislike women, my dear Raleigh, but I know them better than you do, gallant as you are; and when you tell me in one and the same moment that a woman holding absolute sway over men yet lived and died an old maid, you must not be indignant if I smile and bite the end of my thumb, which is the Chinese way of saying that's all in your eye, Betty Martin."

"Believe it or not, you poor old back number," retorted Raleigh, hotly. "It alters nothing. Queen Elizabeth could have married a hundred times over if she had wished. I know I lost my head there completely."

"That shows, Sir Walter," said Dryden, with a grin, "how wrong you are. You lost your head to King James. Hi! Shakespeare, here's a man doesn't know who chopped his head off."

Raleigh's face flushed scarlet. "'Tis better to have had a head and lost it," he cried, "than never to have had a head at all! Mark you, Dryden, my boy, it ill befits you to scoff at me for my misfortune, for dust thou art, and to dust thou hast returned, if word from t'other side about thy books and that which in and on them lies be true."

"Whate'er be said about my books," said Dryden, angrily, "be they read or be they not, 'tis mine they are, and none there be who dare dispute their authorship."

"Thus proving that men, thank Heaven, are still sane," ejaculated Doctor Johnson. "To assume the authorship of Dryden would be not so much a claim, my friend, as a confession."

"Shades of the mighty Chow!" cried Confucius. "An' will ye hear the poets squabble! Egad! A ladies' day could hardly introduce into our midst a more diverting disputation."

"We're all getting a little high-flown in our phraseology," put in Shakespeare at this point. "Let's quit talking in blank-verse and come down to business. *I* think a ladies' day would be great sport. I'll write a poem to read on the occasion."

"Then I oppose it with all my heart," said Doctor Johnson. "Why do you always want to make our entertainments commonplace? Leave occasional poems to mortals. I never knew an occasional poem yet that was worthy of an immortal."

"That's precisely why I want to write one occasional poem. I'd make it worthy," Shakespeare answered. "Like this, for instance:

> *Most   fair,   most   sweet,*
> *most   beauteous   of   ladies,*
> *The greatest charm in all ye*
> *realm of Hades.*

Why, my dear Doctor, such an opportunity for rhyming Hades with ladies should not be lost."

"That just proves what I said," said Johnson. "Any idiot can make ladies rhyme with Hades. It requires absolute genius to avoid the temptation. You are great enough to make Hades rhyme with bicycle if you choose to do it—but no, you succumb to the temptation to be commonplace. Bah! One of these modern drawing-room poets with three sections to his name couldn't do worse."

"On general principles," said Raleigh, "Johnson is right. We invite these people here to see our clubhouse, not to give them an exhibition of our metrical powers, and I think all exercises of a formal nature should be frowned upon."

"Very well," said Shakespeare. "Go ahead. Have your own way about it. Get out your brow and frown. I'm perfectly willing to save myself the trouble of writing a poem. Writing real poetry isn't easy, as you fellows would have discovered for yourselves if you'd ever tried it."

"To pass over the arrogant assumption of the gentleman who has just spoken, with the silence due to a proper expression of our contempt therefor," said Dryden, slowly, "I think in case we do have a ladies' day here we should exercise a most careful supervision over the invitation list. For instance, wouldn't it be awkward for our good friend Henry the Eighth to encounter the various Mrs. Henrys here? Would it not likewise be awkward for them to meet each other?"

"Your point is well taken," said Doctor Johnson. "I don't know whether the King's matrimonial ventures are on speaking terms with each other or not, but under any circumstances it would hardly be a pleasing spectacle for Katharine of Arragon to see Henry running his legs off getting cream and cakes for Anne Boleyn; nor would Anne like it much if, on the other hand, Henry chose to behave like a gentleman and a husband to Jane Seymour or Katharine Parr. I think, if the members themselves are to send out the invitations, they should each be limited to two cards, with the express understanding that no member shall be permitted to invite more than one wife."

"That's going to be awkward," said Raleigh, scratching his head thoughtfully. "Henry is such a hotheaded fellow that he might resent the stipulation."

"I think he would," said Confucius. "I think he'd be as mad as a hatter at your insinuation that he would invite any of his wives, if all I hear of him is true; and what I've heard, Wolsey has told me."

"He knew a thing or two about Henry," said Shakespeare. "If you don't believe it, just read that play of mine that Beaumont and Fletcher—er—ah—thought so much of."

"You came near giving your secret away that time, William," said Johnson, with a sly smile, and giving the Avonian a dig between the ribs.

"Secret! I haven't any secret," said Shakespeare, a little acridly. "It's the truth I'm telling you. Beaumont and Fletcher *did* admire *Henry the Eighth*."

"Thereby showing their conceit, eh?" said Johnson.

"Oh, of course, I didn't write anything, did I?" cried Shakespeare. "Everybody wrote my plays but me. I'm the only person that had no hand in Shakespeare. It seems to me that joke is about worn out, Doctor. I'm getting a little tired of it myself; but if it amuses you, why, keep it up. *I* know who wrote my plays, and whatever you may say cannot affect the facts. Next thing you fellows will be saying that I didn't write my own autographs?"

"I didn't say that," said Johnson, quietly. "Only there is no internal evidence in your autographs that you knew how to spell your name if you did. A man who signs his name Shixpur one day and Shikespeare the next needn't complain if the Bank of Posterity refuses to honor his check."

"They'd honor my check quick enough these days," retorted Shakespeare. "When a man's autograph brings five thousand dollars, or one thousand pounds, in the auction room, there isn't a bank in the world fool enough to decline to honor any check he'll sign under a thousand dollars, or two hundred pounds."

"I fancy you're right," put in Raleigh. "But your checks or your plays have nothing to do with ladies' day. Let's get to some conclusion in this matter."

"Yes," said Confucius. "Let's. Ladies' day is becoming a dreadful bore, and if we don't hurry up the billiard-room will be full."

"Well, I move we get up a petition to the council to have it," said Dryden.

"I agree," said Confucius, "and I'll sign it. If there's one way to avoid having ladies' day in the future, it's to have one now and be done with it."

"All right," said Shakespeare. "I'll sign too."

"As—er—Shixpur or Shikespeare?" queried Johnson.

"Let him alone," said Raleigh. "He's getting sensitive about that; and what you need to learn more than anything else is that it isn't manners to twit a man on facts. What's bothering you, Dryden? You look like a man with an idea."

"It has just occurred to me," said Dryden, "that while we can safely leave the question of Henry the Eighth and his wives to the wisdom of the council, we ought to pay some attention to the advisability of inviting Lucretia Borgia. I'd hate to eat any supper if she came within a mile of the banqueting-hall. If she comes you'll have to appoint a tasting committee before I'll touch a drop of punch or eat a speck of salad."

"We might recommend the appointment of Raleigh to look after the fair Lucretia and see that she has no poison with her, or if she has, to keep her from dropping it into the salads," said Confucius, with a sidelong glance at Raleigh. "He's the especial champion of woman in this club, and no doubt would be proud of the distinction."

"I would with most women," said Raleigh. "But I draw the line at Lucretia Borgia."

And so a petition was drawn up, signed, and sent to the council, and they, after mature deliberation, decided to have the ladies' day, to which all the ladies in Hades, excepting Lucretia Borgia and Delilah, were to be duly invited, only the date was not specified. Delilah was excluded at the request of Samson, whose convincing muscles, rather than his arguments, completely won over all opposition to his proposition.

Lucretia Borgia and Delilah were not invited.

"What is the average weight of a copy of 'Punch'?"
drawled Artemas Ward.

CHAPTER VIII:

A DISCONTENTED SHADE

"IT SEEMS to me," said Shakespeare, wearily, one afternoon at the club—"that this business of being immortal is pretty dull. Didn't somebody once say he'd rather ride fifty years on a trolley in Europe than on a bicycle in Cathay?"

"I never heard any such remark by any self-respecting person," said Johnson.

"I said something like it," observed Tennyson.

Doctor Johnson looked around to see who it was that spoke.

"You?" he cried. "And who, pray, may you be?"

"My name is Tennyson," replied the poet.

"And a very good name it is," said Shakespeare.

"I am not aware that I ever heard the name before," said Doctor Johnson. "Did you make it yourself?"

"I did," said the late laureate, proudly.

"In what pursuit?" asked Doctor Johnson.

"Poetry," said Tennyson. "I wrote 'Locksley Hall' and 'Come into the Garden, Maude.'"

"Humph!" said Doctor Johnson. "I never read 'em."

"Well, why should you have read them?" snarled Carlyle. "They were written after you moved over here, and they were good stuff. You needn't think because you quit, the whole world put up its shutters and went out of business. I did a few things myself which I fancy you never heard of."

"Oh, as for that," retorted Doctor Johnson, with a smile, "I've heard of you; you are the man who wrote the life of Frederick the Great in nine hundred and two volumes—"

"Seven!" snapped Carlyle.

"Well, seven then," returned Johnson. "I never saw the work, but I heard Frederick speaking of it the other day. Bonaparte asked him if he had read it, and Frederick said no, he hadn't time. Bonaparte cried, 'Haven't time? Why, my dear king, you've got all eternity.' 'I know it,' replied Frederick, 'but that isn't enough. Read a page or two, my dear Napoleon, and you'll see why.'"

"Frederick will have his joke," said Shakespeare, with a wink at Tennyson and a smile for the two philosophers, intended, no doubt, to put them in a more agreeable frame of mind. "Why, he even asked me the other day why I never wrote a tragedy about him, completely ignoring the fact that he came along many years after I had departed. I spoke of that, and he said, 'Oh, I was only joking.' I apologized. 'I didn't know that,' said I. 'And why should you?' said he. 'You're English.'"

"A very rude remark," said Johnson. "As if we English were incapable of seeing a joke!"

"Exactly," put in Carlyle. "It strikes me as the absurdest notion that the Englishman can't see a joke. To the mind that is accustomed to snap judgments I have no doubt the Englishman appears to be dull of apprehension, but the philosophy of the whole matter is apparent to the mind that takes the trouble to investigate. The Briton weighs everything carefully before he commits himself, and even though a certain point may strike him as funny, he isn't going to laugh until he has fully made up his mind that it is funny. I remember once riding down Piccadilly with Froude in a hansom cab. Froude had a copy of *Punch* in his hand, and he began to laugh immoderately over something. I leaned over his shoulder to see what he was laughing at. 'That isn't so funny,' said I, as I read the paragraph on which his eye was resting. 'No,' said Froude. 'I wasn't laughing at that. I was enjoying the joke that appeared in the same relative position in last week's issue.' Now that's the point—the whole point. The Englishman always laughs over last week's *Punch*, not this week's, and that is why you will find a file of that interesting journal in the home of all well-to-do Britons. It is the back number that amuses him—which merely proves that he is a deliberative person who weighs even his humor carefully before giving way to his emotions."

"What is the average weight of a copy of *Punch*?" drawled Artemas Ward, who had strolled in during the latter part of the conversation.

Shakespeare snickered quietly, but Carlyle and Johnson looked upon the intruder severely.

"We will take that question into consideration," said Carlyle. "Perhaps tomorrow we shall have a definite answer ready for you."

"Never mind," returned the humorist. "You've proved your point. Tennyson tells me you find life here dull, Shakespeare."

"Somewhat," said Shakespeare. "I don't know about the rest of you fellows, but I was not cut out for an eternity of ease. I must have occupation, and the stage isn't popular here. The trouble about putting on a play here is that our managers are afraid of libel suits. The chances are that if I should write a play with Cassius as the hero, Cassius would go to the first night's performance with a dagger concealed in his toga, with which to punctuate his objections to the lines put in his mouth. There is nothing I'd like better than to manage a theatre in this place, but think of the riots we'd have! Suppose, for an instant, that I wrote a play about Bonaparte! He'd have a box, and when the rest of you spooks called for the author at the end of the third act, if he didn't happen to like the play he'd greet me with a salvo of artillery instead of applause."

"He wouldn't if you made him out a great conqueror from start to finish," said Tennyson.

"No doubt," returned Shakespeare, sadly; "but in that event Wellington would be in the other stage-box, and I'd get the greeting from him."

"Why come out at all?" asked Johnson.

"Why come out at all?" echoed Shakespeare. "What fun is there in writing a play if you can't come out and show yourself at the first night? That's the author's reward. If it wasn't for the first-night business, though, all would be plain sailing."

"Then why don't you begin it the second night?" drawled Ward.

"How the deuce could you?" put in Carlyle.

"A most extraordinary proposition," sneered Johnson.

"Yes," said Ward; "but wait a week—you'll see the point then."

"There isn't any doubt in my mind," said Shakespeare, reverting to his original proposition, "that the only perfectly satisfactory life is under a system not yet adopted in either world—the one we have quitted or this. There we had hard work in which our mortal limitations hampered us grievously; here we have the freedom of the immortal with no hard work; in other words, now that we feel like fighting-cocks, there isn't any fighting to be done. The great life in my estimation, would be to return to earth and battle with mortal problems, but equipped mentally and physically with immortal weapons."

"Some people don't know when they are well off," said Beau Brummel. "This strikes me as being an ideal life. There are no tailors bills to pay—we are ourselves nothing but memories, and a memory can clothe himself in the shadow of his former grandeur—I clothe myself in the remembrance of my departed clothes, and as my memory is good I flatter myself I'm the best-dressed man here. The fact that there are ghosts of departed unpaid bills haunting my bedside at night doesn't bother me in the least, because the bailiffs that in the old life lent terror to an overdue account, thanks to our beneficent system here, are kept in the less agreeable sections of Hades. I used to regret that bailiffs were such low people, but now I rejoice at it. If they had been of a different order they might have proven unpleasant here."

"You are right, my dear Brummel," interposed Munchausen. "This life is far preferable to that in the other sphere. Any of you gentlemen who happen to have had the pleasure of reading my memoirs must have been struck with the tremendous difficulties that encumbered my progress. If I wished for a rare liqueur for my luncheon, a liqueur served only at the table of an Oriental potentate, more jealous of it than of his one thousand queens, I had to raise armies, charter ships, and wage warfare in which feats of incredible valor had to be performed by myself alone and unaided to secure the desired thimbleful. I have destroyed empires for a bon-bon at great expense of nervous energy."

"That's very likely true," said Carlyle. "I should think your feats of strength would have wrecked your imagination in time."

"Not so," said Munchausen. "On the contrary, continuous exercise served only to make it stronger. But, as I was going to say, in this life we have none of these fearful obstacles—it is a life of leisure; and if I want a bird and a cold bottle at any time, instead of placing my life in peril and jeopardizing the peace of all mankind to get it, I have only to summon before me the memory of some previous bird and cold bottle, dine thereon like a well-ordered citizen, and smoke the spirit of the best cigar my imagination can conjure up."

"You miss my point," said Shakespeare. "I don't say this life is worse or better than the other we used to live. What I do say is that a combination of both would suit me. In short, I'd like to live here and go to the other world every day to business, like a suburban resident who sleeps in the country and makes his living in the city. For instance, why shouldn't I dwell here and go to London every day, hire an office there, and put out a sign something like this:

WILLIAM SHAKESPEARE
DRAMATIST

Plays written while you wait

I guess I'd find plenty to do."

"Guess again," said Tennyson. "My dear boy, you forget one thing. *You are out of date.* People don't go to the theatres to hear *you,* they go to see the people who *do* you."

"That is true," said Ward. "And they do do you, my beloved William. It's a wonder to me you are not dizzy turning over in your grave the way they do you."

"Can it be that I can ever be out of date?" asked

Shakespeare. "I know, of course, that I have to be adapted at times; but to be wholly out of date strikes me as a hard fate."

"You're not out of date," interposed Carlyle; "the date is out of you. There is a great demand for Shakespeare in these days, but there isn't any stuff."

"Then I should succeed," said Shakespeare.

"No, I don't think so," returned Carlyle. "You couldn't stand the pace. The world revolves faster today than it did in your time—men write three or four plays at once. This is what you might call a Type-writer Age, and to keep up with the procession you'd have to work as you never worked before."

"That is true," observed Tennyson. "You'd have to learn to be ambidextrous, so that you could keep two type-writing machines going at once; and, to be perfectly frank with you, I cannot even conjure up in my fancy a picture of you knocking out a tragedy with the right hand on one machine, while your left hand is fashioning a farce-comedy on another."

"He might do as a great many modern writers do," said Ward; "go in for the Paper-doll Drama. Cut the whole thing out with a pair of scissors. As the poet might have said if he'd been clever enough:

> *Oh, bring me the scissors,*
> *And bring me the glue,*
> *And a couple of dozen old plays.*
> *I'll cut out and paste*
> *A drama for you*

> *That'll run for quite sixty-two*
> *days.*
>
> *Oh, bring me a dress*
> *Made of satin and lace,*
> *And a book—say Joe Miller's—of*
> *wit;*
>
> *And I'll make the old dramatists*
> *Blue in the face*
> *With the play that I'll turn out for*
> *it.*
>
> *So bring me the scissors,*
> *And bring me the paste,*
> *And a dozen fine old comedies;*
> *A fine line of dresses,*
> *And popular taste*
> *I'll make a strong effort to please.*

"You draw a very blue picture, it seems to me," said Shakespeare, sadly.

"Well, it's true," said Carlyle. "The world isn't at all what it used to be in any one respect, and you fellows who made great reputations centuries ago wouldn't have even the ghost of a show now. I don't believe Homer could get a poem accepted by a modern magazine, and while the comic papers are still printing Diogenes' jokes the old gentleman couldn't make enough out of them in these days to pay taxes on his tub, let alone earning his bread."

"That is exactly so," said Tennyson. "I'd be willing to wager too that, in the line of personal prowess, even D'Artagnan and Athos and Porthos and Aramis couldn't stand London for one day."

"Or New York either," said Mr. Barnum, who had been an interested listener. "A New York policeman could have managed that quartet with one hand."

"Then," said Shakespeare, "in the opinion of you gentlemen, we old-time lions would appear to modern eyes to be more or less stuffed?"

"That's about the size of it," said Carlyle.

"But you'd draw," said Barnum, his face lighting up with pleasure. "You'd drive a five-legged calf to suicide from envy. If I could take you and Cæsar, and Napoleon Bonaparte and Nero over for one circus season we'd drive the mint out of business."

"There's your chance, William," said Ward. "You write a play for Bonaparte and Cæsar, and let Nero take his fiddle and be the orchestra. Under Barnum's management you'd get enough activity in one season to last you through all eternity."

"You can count on me," said Barnum, rising. "Let me know when you've got your plan laid out. I'd stay and make a contract with you now, but Adam has promised to give me points on the management of wild animals without cages, so I can't wait. By-by."

"Humph!" said Shakespeare, as the eminent showman passed out. "That's a gay proposition. When monkeys move in polite society William Shakespeare will make a side-show of himself for a circus."

"They do now," said Thackeray, quietly.

Which merely proved that Shakespeare did not mean what he said; for in spite of Thackeray's insinuation as to the monkeys and polite society, he has not yet accepted the Barnum proposition, though there can be no doubt of its value from the point of view of a circus manager.

Shakespeare as a suburban resident.

CHAPTER IX:

AS TO COOKERY AND SCULPTURE

ROBERT BURNS and Homer were seated at a small table in the dining-room of the houseboat, discussing everything in general and the shade of a very excellent luncheon in particular.

"We are in great luck today," said Burns, as he cut a ruddy duck in twain. "This bird is done just right."

"I agree with you," returned Homer, drawing his chair a trifle closer to the table. "Compared to the one we had here last Thursday, this is a feast for the gods. I wonder who it was that cooked this fowl originally?"

"I give it up; but I suspect it was done by some man who knew his business," said Burns, with a smack of his lips. "It's a pity, I think, my dear Homer, that there is no means by which a cook may become immortal. Cooking is as much of an art as is the writing of poetry, and just as there are immortal poets so there should be immortal cooks. See what an advantage the poet has—

he writes something, it goes out and reaches the inmost soul of the man who reads it, and it is signed. His work is known because he puts his name to it; but this poor devil of a cook—where is he? He has done his work as well as the poet ever did his, it has reached the inmost soul of the mortal who originally ate it, but he cannot get the glory of it because he cannot put his name to it. If the cook could sign his work it would be different."

"You have hit upon a great truth," said Homer, nodding, as he sometimes was wont to do. "And yet I fear that, ingenious as we are, we cannot devise a plan to remedy the matter. I do not know about you, but I should myself much object if my birds and my flapjacks, and other things, digestible and otherwise, that I eat here were served with the cook's name written upon them. An omelet is sometimes a picture—"

"I've seen omelets that looked like one of Turner's sunsets," acquiesced Burns.

"Precisely; and when Turner puts down in one corner of his canvas, 'Turner, fecit,' you do not object, but if the cook did that with the omelet you wouldn't like it."

"No," said Burns; "but he might fasten a tag to it, with his name written upon that."

"That is so," said Homer; "but the result in the end would be the same. The tags would get lost, or perhaps a careless waiter, dropping a tray full of dainties, would get the tags of a good and bad cook mixed in trying to restore the contents of the tray to their previous condition. The tag system would fail."

"There is but one other way that I can think of," said Burns, "and that would do no good now unless we can convey our ideas into the other world; that is, for a great poet to lend his genius to the great cook, and make the latter's name immortal by putting it into a poem. Say, for instance, that you had eaten a fine bit of terrapin, done to the most exquisite point—you could have asked the cook's name, and written an apostrophe to her. Something like this, for instance:

> *Oh, Dinah Rudd! oh, Dinah Rudd!*
> *Thou art a cook of bluest blood!*
> *Nowhere within*
> *This world of sin*
> *Have I e'er tasted better terrapin.*
> *Do you see?"*

"I do; but even then, my dear fellow, the cook would fall short of true fame. Her excellence would be a mere matter of hearsay evidence," said Homer.

"Not if you went on to describe, in a keenly analytical manner, the virtues of that particular bit of terrapin," said Burns. "Draw so vivid a picture of the dish that the reader himself would taste that terrapin even as you tasted it."

"You have hit it!" cried Homer, enthusiastically. "It is a grand plan; but how to introduce it—that is the question."

"We can haunt some modern poet, and give him the idea in that way," suggested Burns. "He will see the novelty of it, and will possibly disseminate the idea as we wish it to be disseminated."

"Done!" said Homer. "I'll begin right away. I feel like haunting tonight. I'm getting to be a pretty old ghost, but I'll never lose my love of haunting."

At this point, as Homer spoke, a fine-looking spirit entered the room, and took a seat at the head of the long table at which the regular club dinner was nightly served.

"Why, bless me!" said Homer, his face lighting up with pleasure. "Why, Phidias, is that you?"

"I think so," said the new-comer, wearily; "at any rate, it's all that's left of me."

"Come over here and lunch with us," said Homer. "You know Burns, don't you?"

"Haven't the pleasure," said Phidias.

The poet and the sculptor were introduced, after which Phidias seated himself at Homer's side.

"Are you any relation to Burns the poet?" the former asked, addressing the Scotchman.

"I *am* Burns the poet," replied the other.

"You don't look much like your statues," said Phidias, scanning his face critically.

"No, thank the Fates!" said Burns, warmly. "If I did, I'd commit suicide."

"Why don't you sue the sculptors for libel?" asked Phidias.

"You speak with a great deal of feeling, Phidias," said Homer, gravely. "Have they done anything to hurt you?"

"They have," said Phidias. "I have just returned from a tour of the world. I have seen the things they call sculpture in these degenerate days, and I must confess—who shouldn't, perhaps—that I could have done better work with a baseball-bat for a chisel and putty for the raw material."

"I think I could do good work with a baseball-bat too," said Burns; "but as for the raw material, give me the heads of the men who have sculped me to work on. I'd leave them so that they'd look like some of your Parthenon frieze figures with the noses gone."

"You are a vindictive creature," said Homer. "These men you criticize, and whose heads you wish to sculpt with a baseball-bat, have done more for you than you ever did for them. Every statue of you these men have made is a standing advertisement of your books, and it hasn't cost you a penny. There isn't a doubt in my mind that if it were not for those statues countless people would go to their graves supposing that the great Scottish Burns were little rivulets, and not a poet. What difference does it make to you if they haven't made an Adonis of you? You never set them an example by making one of yourself. If there's deception anywhere, it isn't you that is deceived; it is the mortals. And who cares about them or their opinions?"

"I never thought of it in that way," said Burns. "I hate caricatures—that is, caricatures of myself. I enjoy caricatures of other people, but—"

"You have a great deal of the mortal left in you, considering that you pose as an immortal," said Homer, interrupting the speaker.

"Well, so have I," said Phidias, resolved to stand by Burns in the argument, "and I'm sorry for the man who hasn't. I was a mortal once, and I'm glad of it. I had a good time, and I don't care who knows it. When I look about me and see Jupiter, the arch-snob of creation, and Mars, a little tin warrior who couldn't have fought a soldier like Napoleon, with all his alleged divinity, I thank the Fates that they enabled me to achieve immortality through mortal effort. Hang hereditary greatness, I say. These men were born immortals. You and I worked for it and got it. We know what it cost. It was ours because we earned it, and not because we were born to it. Eh, Burns?"

The Scotchman nodded assent, and the Greek sculptor went on.

"I am not vindictive myself, Homer," he said. "Nobody has hurt me, and, on the whole, I don't think sculpture is in such a bad way, after all. There's a shoemaker I wot of in the mortal realms who can turn the prettiest last you ever saw; and I encountered a carver in a London eating-house last month who turned out a slice of beef that was cut as artistically as I could have done it myself. What I object to chiefly is the tendency of the times. This is an electrical age, and men in my old profession aren't content to turn out one *chef-d'oeuvre* in a lifetime. They take orders by the gross. I waited upon inspiration. Today the sculptor waits upon custom, and an artist will make a bust of anybody in any material desired as long as he is sure of getting his pay afterwards. I saw a life-size statue of the inventor of a new kind of lard the other day, and what do you suppose the material was? Gold? Not by a great deal. Ivory? Marble, even? Not a bit of it. He was done in lard, sir. I have seen a woman's head done in butter, too, and it makes me distinctly weary to think that my art should be brought so low."

"You did your best work in Greece," chuckled Homer.

"A bad joke, my dear Homer," retorted Phidias. "I thought sculpture was getting down to a pretty low ebb when I had to fashion friezes out of marble; but marble is more precious than rubies alongside of butter and lard."

"Each has its uses," said Homer. "I'd rather have butter on my bread than marble, but I must confess that for sculpture it is very poor stuff, as you say."

"It is indeed," said Phidias. "For practice it's all right to use butter, but for exhibition purposes—bah!"

Here Phidias, to show his contempt for butter as raw material in sculpture, seized a wooden toothpick, and with it modeled a beautiful head of Minerva out of the pat that stood upon the small plate at his side, and before Burns could interfere had spread the chaste figure as thinly as he could upon a piece of bread, which he tossed to the shade of a hungry dog that stood yelping on the river-bank.

"Heavens!" cried Burns. "Imperious Cæsar dead and turned to bricks is as nothing to a Minerva carved by Phidias used to stay the hunger of a ravening cur."

"Well, it's the way I feel," said Phidias, savagely.

"I think you are a trifle foolish to be so eternally vexed about it," said Homer, soothingly. "Of course you feel badly, but, after all, what's the use? You must know that the mortals would pay more for one of your statues than they would for a specimen of any modern sculptor's art; yes, even if yours were modeled in wine-jelly and the other fellow's in pure gold. So why re-pine?"

"You'd feel the same way if poets did a similarly vulgar thing," retorted Phidias; "you know you would. If you should hear of a poet today writing a poem on a thin layer of lard or butter, you would yourself be the first to call a halt."

"No, I shouldn't," said Homer, quietly; "in fact, I wish the poets would do that. We'd have fewer bad poems to read; and that's the way you should look at it. I venture to say that if this modern plan of making busts and friezes in butter had been adopted at an earlier period, the public places in our great cities and our national Walhallas would seem less like repositories of comic art, since the first critical rays of a warm sun would have reduced the carven atrocities therein to a spot on the pavement. The butter school of sculpture has its advantages, my boy, and you should be crowning the inventor of the system with laurel, and not heaping coals of fire upon his brow."

"That," said Burns, "is, after all, the solid truth, Phidias. Take the brass caricatures of me, for instance. Where would they be now if they had been cast in lard instead of in bronze?"

Phidias was silent a moment.

"Well," he said, finally, as the value of the plan dawned upon his mind, "from that point of view I don't know but what you are right, after all; and, to show that I have spoken in no vindictive spirit, let me propose a toast. Here's to the Butter Sculptors. May their butter never give out."

The toast was drained to the dregs, and Phidias went home feeling a little better.

Phidias sees ' a life-size statue
of the inventor of a new kind of lard'.

Phidias modeled a beautiful head of Minerva.

Goldsmith, pale with fear, risks to speak.

CHAPTER X:

STORYTELLERS' NIGHT

IT WAS Storytellers' Night at the houseboat, and the best talkers of Hades were impressed into the service. Doctor Johnson was made chairman of the evening.

"Put him in the chair," said Raleigh. "That's the only way to keep him from telling a story himself. If he starts in on a tale he'll make it a serial sure as fate, but if you make him the medium through which other Storytellers are introduced to the club he'll be finely epigrammatic. He can be very short and sharp when he's talking about somebody else. Personality is his forte."

"Great scheme," said Diogenes, who was chairman of the entertainment committee. "The nights over here are long, but if Johnson started on a story they'd have to reach twice around eternity and halfway back to give him time to finish all he had to say."

"He's not very witty, in my judgment," said Carlyle, who since his arrival in the other world has manifested some jealousy of Solomon and Doctor Johnson.

"That's true enough," said Raleigh; "but he's strong, and he's bound to say something that will put the audience in sympathy with the man that he introduces, and that's half the success of a Storytellers' Night. I've told stories myself. If your audience doesn't sympathize with you you'd be better off at home putting the baby to bed."

And so it happened. Doctor Johnson was made chairman, and the evening came. The Doctor was in great form. A list of the Storytellers had been sent him in advance, and he was prepared. The audience was about as select a one as can be found in Hades. The doors were thrown open to the friends of the members, and the smoke-furnace had been filled with a very superior quality of Arcadian mixture which Scott had brought back from a haunting-trip to the home of "The Little Minister," at Thrums.

"Friends and fellow-spooks," the Doctor began, when all were seated on the visionary camp-stools—which, by the way, are far superior to those in use in a world of realities, because they do not creak in the midst of a fine point demanding absolute silence for appreciation—"I do not know why I have been chosen to preside over this gathering of phantoms; it is the province of the presiding officer on occasions of this sort to say pleasant things, which he does not necessarily endorse, about the sundry persons who are to do the story-telling. Now, I suppose you all know me pretty well by this time. If there is anybody who doesn't, I'll be glad to have him presented after the formal work of the evening is over, and if I don't like him I'll tell him so. You know that if I can be counted upon for any one thing it is candor, and if I hurt the feelings of any of these individuals whom I introduce tonight, I want them distinctly to understand that it is not because I love them less, but that I love truth more. With this—ah—blanket apology, as it were, to cover all possible emergencies that may arise during the evening, I will begin. The first speaker on the program, I regret to observe, is my friend Goldsmith. Affairs of this kind ought to begin with a snap, and while Oliver is a most excellent writer, as a speaker he is a pebbleless Demosthenes. If I had had the arrangement of the program I should have had Goldsmith tell his story while the rest of us were downstairs at supper. However, we must abide by our program, which is unconscionably long, for otherwise we will never get through it. Those of you who agree with me as to the pleasure of listening to my friend Goldsmith will do well to join me in the grill-room while he is speaking, where, I understand, there is a very fine line of punches ready to be served. Modest Noll, will you kindly inflict yourself upon the gathering, and send me word when you get through, if you ever do, so that I may return and present number two to the assembly, whoever or whatever he may be?"

With these words the Doctor retired, and poor Goldsmith, pale with fear, rose up to speak. It was evident that he was quite as doubtful of his ability as a talker as was Johnson.

"I'm not much of a talker, or, as some say, speaker,"

he said. "Talking is not my forte, as Doctor Johnson has told you, and I am therefore not much at it. Speaking is not in my line. I cannot speak or talk, as it were, because I am not particularly ready at the making of a speech, due partly to the fact that I am not much of a talker anyhow, and seldom if ever speak. I will therefore not bore you by attempting to speak, since a speech by one who like myself is, as you are possibly aware, not a fluent nor indeed in any sense an eloquent speaker, is apt to be a bore to those who will be kind enough to listen to my remarks, but will read instead the first five chapters of the *Vicar of Wakefield*."

"Who suggested any such night as this, anyhow?" growled Carlyle. "Five chapters of the *Vicar of Wakefield* for a starter! Lord save us, we'll need a Vicar of Sleepfield if he's allowed to do this!"

"I move we adjourn," said Darwin.

"Can't something be done to keep these younger members quiet?" asked Solomon, frowning upon Carlyle and Darwin.

"Yes," said Douglas Jerrold. "Let Goldsmith go on. He'll have them asleep in ten minutes."

Meanwhile, Goldsmith was plodding earnestly through his stint, utterly and happily oblivious of the effect he was having upon his audience.

"This is awful," whispered Wellington to Bonaparte.

"Worse than Waterloo," replied the ex-Emperor, with a grin; "but we can stop it in a minute. Artemas Ward told me once how a camp-meeting he attended in the West broke up to go outside and see a dog-fight.

Can't you and I pretend to quarrel? A personal assault by you on me will wake these people up and discombobulate Goldsmith. Say the word—only don't hit too hard."

"I'm with you," said Wellington. Whereupon, with a great show of heat, he roared out, "You? Never! I'm more afraid of a boy with a bean-snapper that I ever was of you!" and followed up his remark by pulling Bonaparte's camp-chair from under him, and letting the conqueror of Austerlitz fall to the floor with a thud which I have since heard described as dull and sickening.

The effect was instantaneous. Compared to a personal encounter between the two great figures of Waterloo, a reading from his own works by Goldsmith seemed lacking in the elements essential to the holding of an audience. Consequently, attention was centred in the belligerent warriors, and, by some odd mistake, when a peace-loving member of the assemblage, realizing the indecorousness of the incident, cried out, "Put him out! put him out!" the attendants rushed in, and, taking poor Goldsmith by his collar, hustled him out through the door, across the deck, and tossed him ashore without reference to the gang-plank. This accomplished, a personal explanation of their course was made by the quarrelling generals, and, peace having been restored, a committee was sent in search of Goldsmith with suitable apologies. The good and kindly soul returned, but having lost his book in the mêlée, much to his own gratification, as well as to that of the audience, he was permitted to rest in quiet the balance of the evening.

"Is he through?" said Johnson, poking his head in at the door when order was restored.

"Yes, sir," said Boswell; "that is to say, he has retired permanently from the field. He didn't finish, though."

"Fellow-spooks," began Johnson once more, "now that you have been delighted with the honeyed eloquence of the last speaker, it is my privilege to present to you that eminent fabulist Baron Munchausen, the greatest unrealist of all time, who will give you an exhibition of his paradoxical power of lying while standing."

The applause which greeted the Baron was deafening. He was, beyond all doubt, one of the most popular members of the club.

"Speaking of whales," said he, leaning gracefully against the table.

"Nobody has mentioned 'em," said Johnson.

"True," retorted the Baron; "but you always suggest them by your apparently unquenchable thirst for spouting—speaking of whales, my friend Jonah, as well as the rest of you, may be interested to know that I once had an experience similar to his own, and, strange to say, with the identical whale."

Jonah arose from his seat in the back of the room. "I do not wish to be unpleasant," he said, with a strong effort to be calm, "but I wish to ask if Judge Blackstone is in the room."

"I am," said the Judge, rising. "What can I do for

you?"

"I desire to apply for an injunction restraining the Baron from using my whale in his story. That whale, your honor, is copyrighted," said Jonah. "If I had any other claim to the affection of mankind than the one which is based on my experience with that leviathan, I would willingly permit the Baron to introduce him into his story; but that whale, your honor, is my stock in trade—he is my all."

"I think Jonah's point is well taken," said Blackstone, turning to the Baron. "It would be a distinct hardship, I think, if the plaintiff in this action were to be deprived of the exclusive use of his sole accessory. The injunction prayed for is therefore granted. The court would suggest, however, that the Baron continue with his story, using another whale for the purpose."

"It is impossible," said Munchausen, gloomily. "The whole point of the story depends upon its having been Jonah's whale. Under the circumstances, the only thing I can do is to sit down. I regret the narrowness of mind exhibited by my friend Jonah, but I must respect the decision of the court."

"I must take exception to the Baron's allusion to my narrowness of mind," said Jonah, with some show of heat. "I am simply defending my rights, and I intend to continue to do so if the whole world unites in considering my mind a mere slot scarcely wide enough for the insertion of a nickel. That whale was my discovery, and the personal discomfort I endured in perfecting my experience was such that I resolved to rest my reputation upon his broad proportions only—to sink or swim with him—and I cannot at this late day permit another to crowd me out of his exclusive use."

Jonah sat down and fanned himself, and the Baron, with a look of disgust on his face, left the room.

"Up to his old tricks," he growled as he went. "He queers everything he goes into. If I'd known he was a member of this club I'd never have joined."

"We do not appear to be progressing very rapidly," said Doctor Johnson, rising. "So far we have made two efforts to have stories told, and have met with disaster each time. I don't know but what you are to be congratulated, however, on your escape. Very few of you, I observe, have as yet fallen asleep. The next number on the program, I see, is Boswell, who was to have entertained you with a few reminiscences; I say was to have done so, because he is not to do so."

"I'm ready," said Boswell, rising.

"No doubt," retorted Johnson, severely, "but I am not. You are a man with one subject—myself. I admit it's a good subject, but you are not the man to treat of it—here. You may suffice for mortals, but here it is different. I can speak for myself. You can go out and sit on the banks of the Vitriol Reservoir and lecture to the imps if you want to, but when it comes to reminiscences of me I'm on deck myself, and I flatter myself I remember what I said and did more accurately than you do. Therefore, gentlemen, instead of listening to Boswell at this point, you will kindly excuse him and listen to me. Ahem! When I was a boy—"

"Excuse me," said Solomon, rising; "about how long is this—ah—this entertaining discourse of yours to continue?"

"Until I get through," returned Johnson, wrathfully.

"Are you aware, sir, that I am on the program?" asked Solomon.

"I am," said the Doctor. "With that in mind, for the sake of our fellow-spooks who are present, I am very much inclined to keep on forever. When I was a boy—"

Carlyle rose up at this point.

"I should like to ask," he said, mildly, "if this is supposed to be an audience of children? I, for one, have no wish to listen to the juvenile stories of Doctor Johnson. Furthermore, I have come here particularly tonight to hear Boswell. I want to compare him with Froude. I therefore protest against—"

"There is a roof to this houseboat," said Doctor Johnson. "If Mr. Carlyle will retire to the roof with Boswell I have no doubt he can be accommodated. As for Solomon's interruption, I can afford to pass that over with the silent contempt it deserves, though I may add with propriety that I consider his most famous proverbs the most absurd bits of hack-work I ever encountered; and as for that story about dividing a baby between two mothers by splitting it in two, it was grossly inhuman unless the baby was twins. When I was a boy—"

As the Doctor proceeded, Carlyle and Solomon, accompanied by the now angry Boswell, left the room, and my account of the Storytellers' Night must perforce stop; because, though I have never heretofore confessed it, all my information concerning the houseboat on the Styx has been derived from the memoranda of Boswell. It may be interesting to the reader to learn, however, that, according to Boswell's account, the Storytellers' Night was never finished; but whether this means that it broke up immediately afterwards in a riot, or that Doctor Johnson is still at work detailing his reminiscences, I am not aware, and I cannot at the moment of writing ascertain, for Boswell, when I have the pleasure of meeting him, invariably avoids the subject.

Wellington pulls Bonaparte's camp chair
from under him.

CHAPTER XI:

AS TO SAURIANS AND OTHERS

IT WAS Noah who spoke.

"I'm glad," he said, "that when I embarked at the time of the heavy rains that did so much damage in the old days, there weren't any dogs like that fellow Cerberus about. If I'd had to feed a lot of three-headed beasts like him the Ark would have run short of provisions inside of ten days."

"That's very likely true," observed Mr. Barnum; "but I must confess, my dear Noah, that you showed a lamentable lack of the showman's instinct when you selected the animals you did. A more commonplace lot of beasts were never gathered together, and while Adam is held responsible for the introduction of sin into the world, I attribute most of my offences to none other than yourself."

The members of the club drew their chairs a little closer. The conversation had opened a trifle spicily, and, furthermore, they had retained enough of their mortality to be interested in animal stories. Adam, who had managed to settle his back dues and delinquent house-charges, and once more acquired the privileges of the club, nodded his head gratefully at Mr. Barnum.

"I'm glad to find someone," said he, "who places the responsibility for trouble where it belongs. I'm round-shouldered with the blame I've had to bear. I didn't invent sin any more than I invented the telephone, and I think it's rather rough on a fellow who lived a quiet, retiring, pastoral life, minding his own business and staying home nights, to be held up to public reprobation for as long a time as I have."

"It'll be all right in time," said Raleigh; "just wait—be patient, and your vindication will come. Nobody thought much of the plays Bacon and I wrote for Shakespeare until Shakespeare 'd been dead a century."

"Humph!" said Adam, gloomily. "Wait! What have I been doing all this time? I've waited all the time there's been so far, and until Mr. Barnum spoke as he did I haven't observed the slightest inclination on the part of anybody to rehabilitate my lost reputation. Nor do I see exactly how it's to come about even if I do wait."

"You might apply for an investigating committee to look into the charges," suggested an American politician, just over. "Get your friends on it, and you'll be all right."

"Better let sleeping dogs lie," said Blackstone.

"I intend to," said Adam. "The fact is, I hate to give any further publicity to the matter. Even if I did bring the case into court and sue for libel, I've only got one witness to prove my innocence, and that's my wife. I'm not going to drag her into it. She's got nervous prostration over her position as it is, and this would make it worse. Queen Elizabeth and the rest of these snobs in society won't invite her to any of their functions because they say she hadn't any grandfather; and even if she were received by them, she'd be uncomfortable going about. It isn't pleasant for a woman to feel that everyone knows she's the oldest woman in the room."

"Well, take my word for it," said Raleigh, kindly. "It'll all come out all right. You know the old saying, 'History repeats itself.' Some day you will be living back in Eden again, and if you are only careful to make an exact record of all you do, and have a notary present, before whom you can make an affidavit as to the facts, you will be able to demonstrate your innocence."

"I was only condemned on hearsay evidence, anyhow," said Adam, ruefully.

"Nonsense; you were caught red-handed," said Noah; "my grandfather told me so. And now that I've got a chance to slip in a word edgewise, I'd like mightily to have you explain your statement, Mr. Barnum, that I am responsible for your errors. That is a serious charge to bring against a man of my reputation."

"I mean simply this: that to make a show interesting," said Mr. Barnum, "a man has got to provide interesting materials, that's all. I do not mean to say a word that is in any way derogatory to your morality. You were a surprisingly good man for a sea-captain, and with the exception of that one occasion when you—

ah—you allowed yourself to be stranded on the bar, if I may so put it, I know of nothing to be said against you as a moral, temperate person."

"That was only an accident," said Noah, reddening. "You can't expect a man six hundred odd years of age—"

"Certainly not," said Raleigh, soothingly, "and nobody thinks less of you for it. Considering how you must have hated the sight of water, the wonder of it is that it didn't become a fixed habit. Let us hear what it is that Mr. Barnum does criticize in you."

"His taste, that's all," said Mr. Barnum. "I contend that, compared to the animals he might have had, the ones he did have were as ant-hills to Alps. There were more magnificent zoos allowed to die out through Noah's lack of judgment than one likes to think of. Take the Proterosaurus, for instance. Where on earth do we find his equal today?"

"You ought to be mighty glad you can't find one like him," put in Adam. "If you'd spent a week in the Garden of Eden with me, with lizards eight feet long dropping out of the trees on to your lap while you were trying to take a Sunday-afternoon nap, you'd be willing to dispense with things of that sort for the balance of your natural life. If you want to get an idea of that experience let somebody drop a calf on you some afternoon."

"I am not saying anything about that," returned Barnum. "It would be unpleasant to have an elephant drop on one after the fashion of which you speak, but I am glad the elephant was saved just the same. I haven't advocated the Proterosaurus as a Sunday-afternoon surprise, but as an attraction for a show. I still maintain that a lizard as big as a cow would prove a lodestone, the drawing powers of which the pocket-money of the small boy would be utterly unable to resist. Then there was the Iguanadon. He'd have brought a fortune to the box-office—"

"Which you'd have immediately lost," retorted Noah, "paying rent. When you get a reptile of his size, that reaches thirty feet up into the air when he stands on his hind-legs, the ordinary circus wagon of commerce can't be made to hold him, and your menagerie-room has to have ceilings so high that every penny he brought to the box-office would be spent storing him."

"Mischievous, too," said Adam, "that Iguanadon. You couldn't keep anything out of his reach. We used to forbid animals of his kind to enter the garden, but that didn't bother him; he'd stand up on his hind-legs and reach over and steal anything he'd happen to want."

"I could have used him for a fire-escape," said Mr. Barnum; "and as for my inability to provide him with quarters, I'd have met that problem after a short while. I've always lamented the absence, too, of the Megalosaurus—"

"Which simply shows how ignorant you are," retorted Noah. "Why, my dear fellow, it would have taken the whole of an ordinary zoo such as yours to give the Megalosaurus a lunch. Those fellows would eat a rhinoceros as easily as you'd crack a peanut. I did have a couple of Megalosaurians on my boat for just twenty-four hours, and then I chucked them both overboard. If I'd kept them ten days longer they'd have eaten every blessed beast I had with me, and your Zoo wouldn't have had anything else but Megalosaurians."

"Papa is right about that, Mr. Barnum," said Shem. "The whole Saurian tribe was a fearful nuisance. About four hundred years before the flood I had a pet Creosaurus that I kept in our barn. He was a cunning little devil—full of tricks, and all that; but we never could keep a cow or a horse on the place while he was about. They'd mysteriously disappear, and we never knew what became of 'em until one morning we surprised Fido in—"

"Surprised who?" asked Doctor Johnson, scornfully.

"Fido," returned Shem. "'That was my Creosaurus's name."

"Lord save us! Fido!" cried Johnson. "What a name for a Creosaurus!"

"Well, what of it?" asked Shem, angrily. "You wouldn't have us call a mastodon like that Fanny, would you, or Tatters?"

"Go on," said Johnson; "I've nothing to say."

"Shall I send for a physician?" put in Boswell, looking anxiously at his chief, the situation was so extraordinary.

Solomon and Carlyle giggled; and the Doctor having politely requested Boswell to go to a warmer section of the country, Shem resumed.

"I caught him in the act of swallowing five cows

and Ham's favorite trotter, sulky and all."

Baron Munchausen rose up and left the room.

"If they're going to lie I'm going to get out," he said, as he passed through the room.

"What became of Fido?" asked Boswell.

"The sulky killed him," returned Shem, innocently. "He couldn't digest the wheels."

Noah looked approvingly at his son, and, turning to Barnum, observed, quietly:

"What he says is true, and I will go further and say that it is my belief that you would have found the show business impossible if I had taken that sort of creature aboard. You'd have got mightily discouraged after your Antediluvians had chewed up a few dozen steam calliopes, and eaten every other able-bodied exhibit you had managed to secure. I'd have tried to save a couple of Discosaurians if I hadn't supposed they were able to take care of themselves. A combination of sea-serpent and dragon, with a neck twenty-two feet long, it seemed to me, ought to have been able to ride out any storm or fall of rain; but there I was wrong, and I am free to admit my error. It never occurred to me that the sea-serpents were in any danger, so I let them alone, with the result that I never saw but one other, and he was only an illusion due to that unhappy use of stimulants to which, with shocking bad taste, you have chosen to refer."

"I didn't mean to call up unpleasant memories," said Barnum. "I never believed you got half-seas over, anyhow; but, to return to our muttons, why didn't you hand down a few varieties of the Therium family to posterity? There were the Dinotherium and the Megatherium, either one of which would have knocked spots out of any leopard that ever was made, and along side of which even my woolly horse would have paled into insignificance. That's what I can't understand in your selections; with Megatheriums to burn, why save leopards and panthers and other such every-day creatures?"

"What kind of a boat do you suppose I had?" cried Noah. "Do you imagine for a moment that she was four miles on the water-line, with a mile and three-quarters beam? If I'd had a pair of Dinotheriums in the stern of that Ark, she'd have tipped up fore and aft, until she'd have looked like a telegraph-pole in the water, and if I'd put 'em amidships they'd have had to be wedged in so tightly they couldn't move to keep the vessel trim. I didn't go to sea, my friend, for the purpose of being tipped over in mid-ocean every time one of my cargo wanted to shift his weight from one leg to the other."

"It was bad enough with the elephants, wasn't it, papa?" said Shem.

"Yes, indeed, my son," returned the patriarch. "It was bad enough with the elephants. We had to shift our ballast half a dozen times a day to keep the boat from travelling on her beam ends, the elephants moved about so much; and when we came to the question of provender, it took up about nine-tenths of our hold to store hay and peanuts enough to keep them alive and good-tempered. On the whole, I think it's rather late in the day, considering the trouble I took to save anything but myself and my family, to be criticized as I now am. You ought to be much obliged to me for saving any animals at all. Most people in my position would have built a yacht for themselves and family, and let everything else slide."

"That is quite true," observed Raleigh, with a pacificatory nod at Noah. "You were eminently unselfish, and while, with Mr. Barnum, I exceedingly regret that the Saurians and Therii and other tribes were left on the pier when you sailed, I nevertheless think that you showed most excellent judgment at the time."

"He was the only man who had any at all, for that matter," suggested Shem, "and it required all his courage to show it. Everybody was guying him. Sinners stood around the yard all day and every day, criticizing the model; one scoffer pretended he thought her a canalboat, and asked how deep the flood was likely to be on the tow-path, and whether we intended to use mules in shallow water and giraffes in deep; another asked what time allowance we expected to get in a fifteen-mile run, and hinted that a year and two months per mile struck him as being the proper thing—"

"It was far from pleasant," said Noah, tapping his fingers together reflectively. "I don't want to go through it again, and if, as Raleigh suggests, history is likely to repeat herself, I'll sublet the contract to Barnum here, and let him get the chaff."

"It was all right in the end, though, dad," said Shem. "We had the great laugh on 'hoi polloi' the second day out."

"We did, indeed," said Noah. "When we told 'em we only carried first-class passengers and had no room for emigrants, they began to see that the Ark wasn't such an old tub, after all; and a good ninety per cent. of them would have given ten dollars for a little of that time allowance they'd been talking to us about for several centuries."

Noah lapsed into a musing silence, and Barnum rose to leave.

"I still wish you'd saved a Discosaurus," he said. "A creature with a neck twenty-two feet long would have been a gold mine to me. He could have been trained to stand in the ring, and by stretching out his neck bite the little boys who sneak in under the tent and occupy seats on the top row."

"Well, for your sake," said Noah, with a smile, "I'm very sorry; but for my own, I'm quite satisfied with the general results."

And they all agreed that the patriarch had every reason to be pleased with himself.

"Papa is right about that, Mr. Barnum," said Shem.

I'd like mightily to have you explain
your statement, Mr.Barnum."

CHAPTER XII:

THE HOUSEBOAT DISAPPEARS

QUEEN ELIZABETH, attended by Ophelia and Xanthippe, was walking along the river-bank. It was a beautiful autumn day, although, owing to certain climatic peculiarities of Hades, it seemed more like midsummer. The mercury in the club thermometer was nervously clicking against the top of the crystal tube, and poor Cerberus was having all he could do with his three mouths snapping up the pestiferous little shades of by-gone gnats that seemed to take an almost unholy pleasure in alighting upon his various noses and ears.

Ophelia was doing most of the talking.

"I am sure I have never wished to ride one of them," she said, positively. "In the first place, I do not see where the pleasure of it comes in, and, in the second, it seems to me as if skirts must be dangerous. If they should catch in one of the pedals, where would I be?"

"In the hospital shortly, methinks," said Queen Elizabeth.

"Well, I shouldn't wear skirts," snapped Xanthippe. "If a man's wife can't borrow some of her husband's clothing to reduce her peril to a minimum, what is the use of having a husband? When I take to the bicycle, which, in spite of all Socrates can say, I fully intend to do, I shall have a man's wheel, and I shall wear Socrates' old dress clothes. If Hades doesn't like it, Hades may suffer."

"I don't see how Socrates' clothes will help you," observed Ophelia. "He wore skirts himself, just like all the other old Greeks. His toga would be quite as apt to catch in the gear as your skirts."

Xanthippe looked puzzled for a moment. It was evident that she had not thought of the point which Ophelia had brought up—strong-minded ladies of her kind are apt sometimes to overlook important links in such chains of evidence as they feel called upon to use in binding themselves to their rights.

"The women of your day were relieved of that dress problem, at any rate," laughed Queen Elizabeth.

"The women of my day," retorted Xanthippe, "in matters of dress were the equals of their husbands—in my family particularly; now they have lost their rights, and are made to confine themselves still to garments like those of yore, while man has arrogated to himself the sole and exclusive use of sane habiliments. However, that is apart from the question. I was saying that I shall have a man's wheel, and shall wear Socrates' old dress-clothes to ride it in, if Socrates has to go out and buy an old dress-suit for the purpose."

The Queen arched her brows and looked inquiringly at Xanthippe for a moment.

"A magnificent old maid was lost to the world when you married," she said. "Feeling as you do about men, my dear Xanthippe, I don't see why you ever took a husband."

"Humph!" retorted Xanthippe. "Of course you don't. You didn't need a husband. You were born with something to govern. I wasn't."

"How about your temper?" suggested Ophelia, meekly.

Xanthippe sniffed frigidly at this remark.

"I never should have gone crazy over a man if I'd remained unmarried forty thousand years," she retorted, severely. "I married Socrates because I loved him and admired his sculpture; but when he gave up sculpture and became a thinker he simply tried me beyond all endurance, he was so thoughtless, with the result that, having ventured once or twice to show my natural resentment, I have been handed down to posterity as a shrew. I've never complained, and I don't complain now; but when a woman is married to a philosopher who is so taken up with his studies that when he rises in the morning he doesn't look what he is doing, and goes off to his business in his wife's clothes, I think she is entitled to a certain amount of sympathy."

"And yet you wish to wear his," persisted Ophelia.

"Turn about is fair-play," said Xanthippe. "I've suffered so much on his account that on the principle of averages he deserves to have a little drop of bitters in his nectar."

"You are simply the victim of man's deceit," said Elizabeth, wishing to mollify the now angry Xanthippe, who was on the verge of tears. "I understood men, fortunately, and so never married. I knew my father, and even if I hadn't been a wise enough child to know him, I should not have wed, because he married enough to last one family for several years."

"You must have had a hard time refusing all those lovely men, though," sighed Ophelia. "Of course, Sir Walter wasn't as handsome as my dear Hamlet, but he was very fetching."

"I cannot deny that," said Elizabeth, "and I didn't really have the heart to say no when he asked me; but I did tell him that if he married me I should not become Mrs. Raleigh, but that he should become King Elizabeth. He fled to Virginia on the next steamer. My diplomacy rid me of a very unpleasant duty."

Chatting thus, the three famous spirits passed slowly along the path until they came to the sheltered nook in which the houseboat lay at anchor.

"There's a case in point," said Xanthippe, as the houseboat loomed up before them. "All that luxury is for men; we women are not permitted to cross the gangplank. Our husbands and brothers and friends go there; the door closes on them, and they are as completely lost to us as though they never existed. We don't know what goes on in there. Socrates tells me that their amusements are of a most innocent nature, but how do I know what he means by that? Furthermore, it keeps him from home, while I have to stay at home and be entertained by my sons, whom the Encyclopedia Britannica rightly calls dull and fatuous. In other words, club life for him, and dullness and fatuity for me."

"I think myself they're rather queer about letting women into that boat," said Queen Elizabeth. "But it isn't Sir Walter's fault. He told me he tried to have them establish a Ladies' Day, and that they agreed to do so, but have since resisted all his efforts to have a date set for the function."

"It would be great fun to steal in there now, wouldn't it," giggled Ophelia. "There doesn't seem to be anybody about to prevent our doing so."

"That's true," said Xanthippe. "All the windows are closed, as if there wasn't a soul there. I've half a mind to take a peep in at the house."

"I am with you," said Elizabeth, her face lighting up with pleasure. It was a great novelty, and an unpleasant one to her, to find someplace where she could not go. "Let's do it," she added.

So the three women tiptoed softly up the gangplank, and, silently boarding the houseboat, peeped in at the windows. What they saw merely whetted their curiosity.

"I must see more," cried Elizabeth, rushing around to the door, which opened at her touch. Xanthippe and Ophelia followed close on her heels, and shortly they found themselves, open-mouthed in wondering admiration, in the billiard-room of the floating palace, and Richard, the ghost of the best billiard-room attendant in or out of Hades, stood before them.

"Excuse me," he said, very much upset by the sudden apparition of the ladies. "I'm very sorry, but ladies are not admitted here."

"We are equally sorry," retorted Elizabeth, assuming her most imperious manner, "that your masters have seen fit to prohibit our being here; but, now that we are here, we intend to make the most of the opportunity, particularly as there seem to be no members about. What has become of them all?"

Richard smiled broadly. "I don't know where they are," he replied; but it was evident that he was not telling the exact truth.

"Oh, come, my boy," said the Queen, kindly, "you do know. Sir Walter told me you knew everything. Where are they?"

"Well, if you must know, ma'am," returned Richard, captivated by the Queen's manner, "they've all gone down the river to see a prize-fight between Goliath and Samson."

"See there!" cried Xanthippe. "That's what this club makes possible. Socrates told me he was coming here to take luncheon with Carlyle, and they've both of 'em gone off to a disgusting prize-fight!"

"Yes, ma'am, they have," said Richard; "and if Goliath wins, I don't think Mr. Socrates will get home this evening."

"Betting, eh?" said Xanthippe, scornfully.

"Yes, ma'am," returned Richard.

"More club!" cried Xanthippe.

"Oh no, ma'am," said Richard. "Betting is not allowed in the club; they're very strict about that. But the shore is only ten feet off, ma'am, and the gentlemen always go ashore and make their bets."

During this little colloquy Elizabeth and Ophelia were wandering about, admiring everything they saw.

"I do wish Lucretia Borgia and Calpurnia could see this. I wonder if the Cæsars are on the telephone," Elizabeth said. Investigation showed that both the Borgias and the Cæsars were on the wire, and in short order the two ladies had been made acquainted with the state of affairs at the houseboat; and as they were both quite as anxious to see the interior of the much-talked-of club-house as the others, they were not long in arriving. Furthermore, they brought with them half a dozen more ladies, among whom were Desdemona and Cleopatra, and then began the most extraordinary session the houseboat ever knew. A meeting was called, with Elizabeth in the chair, and all the best ladies of the Stygian realms were elected members. Xanthippe, amid the greatest applause, moved that every male member of the organization be expelled for conduct unworthy of a gentleman in attending a prize-fight, and encouraging two such horrible creatures as Goliath and Samson in their nefarious pursuits. Desdemona seconded the motion, and it was carried without a dissenting voice, although Mrs. Cæsar, with becoming dignity, merely smiled approval, not caring to take part too actively in the proceedings.

The men having thus been disposed of in a summary

fashion, Richard was elected janitor in Charon's place, and the club was entirely reorganized, with Cleopatra as permanent President. The meeting then adjourned, and the invaders set about enjoying their newly acquired privileges. The smoking-room was thronged for a few moments, but owing to the extraordinary strength of the tobacco which the faithful Richard shoveled into the furnace, it developed no enduring popularity, Xanthippe, with a suddenly acquired pallor, being the first to renounce the pastime as revolting.

So fast and furious was the enjoyment of these thirsty souls, so long deprived of their rights, that night came on without their observing it, and with the night was brought the great peril into which they were thrown, and from which at the moment of writing they had not been extricated, and which, to my regret, has cut me off for the present from any further information connected with the Associated Shades and their beautiful lounging-place. Had they not been so intent upon the inner beauties of the Houseboat on the Styx they might have observed approaching, under the shadow of the westerly shore, a long, rakish craft propelled by oars, which dipped softly and silently and with trained precision in the now jet-black waters of the Styx. Manning the oars were a dozen evil-visaged ruffians, while in the stern of the approaching vessel there sat a grim-faced, weather-beaten spirit, armed to the teeth, his coat sleeves bearing the skull and cross-bones, the insignia of piracy.

This boat, stealing up the river like a thief in the

night, contained Captain Kidd and his pirate crew, and their mission was a mission of vengeance. To put the matter briefly and plainly, Captain Kidd was smarting under the indignity which the club had recently put upon him. He had been unanimously blackballed, even his proposer and seconder, who had been browbeaten into nominating him for membership, voting against him.

"I may be a pirate," he cried, when he heard what the club had done, "but I have feelings, and the Associated Shades will repent their action. The time will come when they'll find that I have their clubhouse, and they have—its debts."

It was for this purpose that the great terror of the seas had come upon this, the first favorable opportunity. Kidd knew that the houseboat was unguarded; his spies had told him that the members had every one gone to the fight, and he resolved that the time had come to act. He did not know that the Fates had helped to make his vengeance all the more terrible and withering by putting the most attractive and fashionable ladies of the Stygian country likewise in his power; but so it was, and they, poor souls, while this fiend, relentless and cruel, was slowly approaching, sang on and danced on in blissful unconsciousness of their peril.

In less than five minutes from the time when his sinister-craft rounded the bend Kidd and his crew had boarded the houseboat, cut her loose from her moorings, and in ten minutes she had sailed away into the great unknown, and with her went some of the most precious gems in the social diadem of Hades.

The rest of my story is soon told. The whole country was aroused when the crime was discovered, but up to the date of this narrative no word has been received of the missing craft and her precious cargo. Raleigh and Cæsar have had the seas scoured in search of her, Hamlet has offered his kingdom for her return, but unavailingly; and the men of Hades were cast into a gloom from which there seems to be no relief.

Socrates alone was unaffected.

"They'll come back some day, my dear Raleigh," he said, as the knight buried his face, weeping, in his hands. "So why repine? I'll never lose my Xanthippe—permanently, that is. I know that, for I am a philosopher, and I know there is no such thing as luck. And we can start another club."

"Very likely," sighed Raleigh, wiping his eyes. "I don't mind the club so much, but to think of those poor women—"

"Oh, they're all right," returned Socrates, with a laugh. "Cæsar's wife is along, and you can't dispute the fact that she's a good chaperone. Give the ladies a chance. They've been after our club for years; now let 'em have it, and let us hope that they like it. Order me up a hemlock sour, and let's drink to their enjoyment of club life."

Which was done, and I, in spirit, drank with them, for I sincerely hope that the "New Women" of Hades are having a good time.

The fair strollers

It was Captain Kidd and his pirate crew.

JOHN KENDRICK BANGS (May 27, 1862 – January 21, 1922) was an American author, humorist, editor and satirist. His style came to be known as Bangsian fantasy, a fantasy genre in which famous literary or historical individuals interact in the afterlife.

***

Did you enjoy this book? Then please be a sport and give it a good review.

Good reviews help us, which helps our authors. This particular book may be public domain, but only you can help bring attention to us and our authors who are, in fact, still alive and desperately craving attention.

***

Find more titles by the Writers of the Apocalypse at:
http://woksprint.apocalypsewriters.com

www.ingramcontent.com/pod-product-compliance
Lightning Source LLC
Chambersburg PA
CBHW060804210726
48292CB00013B/1762